Prison Pen Pal

Luna May

Contents

Chapter 1

I t is 6:00 pm and I have just got off my shift at work. My feet hurt from the constant running around with patients and my head hurts from the amount of screaming babies that I came across today. Usually, being a pediatric nurse is my favorite thing in my life, but today was weirdly exhausting. I walk through the front door of my two bedroom apartment, kick off my shoes, and set my purse down on the granite countertop. My 3 year old german shepherd, Rufus, gets out of his plush dog bed and runs to greet me. I bend down, kiss Rufus on the nose, and give him scratches behind his ears.

Rufus has been my companion through everything that has happened to me the past few years. Two years ago, my parents got into a sudden car crash and were killed on site. I had been in my junior year of nursing school at the time, and I felt completely alone and lost. My brother, Dave, couldn't deal so he moved from our hometown of Seattle, all the way to Florida. I tried not to take him moving personally, but it's hard to imagine him moving across the country for any other reason other than getting away from his old life. I try to call him every month, but it always goes to voicemail. Thankfully, my aunt Ruby, my best friend Kiera, her girlfriend Michelle, and Rufus had my back that year. They helped me heal in ways I couldn't have alone.

I walk into my crisp white bedroom, pick up my small watering can from the side of the room and water my plant babies that hang by the window. Then, I change out of my light pink scrubs, and put on some black sweats and a grey, oversized sweatshirt. Throwing my scrubs into the hamper, I trudge into my connected bathroom and put my light blonde hair into a topknot. I lean over the counter on my elbows and stare at myself in the mirror. I am so alone. Kiera is currently out of town on a business trip, Michelle is dealing with a crazy case at her law firm, and Aunt Ruby lives in New York which means it's around 11pm over there. Maybe even though Kiera is out I could call her. I shut off the bathroom light and walk into the kitchen. Grabbing my phone out of my purse, I press on Kiera Ackerman and fall backwards onto the couch. After a few seconds of ringing, Kiera picks up.

"Hey Lucy! What are you up too?" Her cheery voice echos over the phone. I smile and sigh.

"Kiera hey! I just wanted to check in on how you're doing, I'm lonely without you." I hear her slightly giggle.

"I am having so much fun in Atlanta. The women engineers conference has actually been really interesting. I'm getting a ton of ideas of things I can implement at my civil engineering job at home."

"That sounds great Kiera, have you met any new women engineers you like?"

"Yes! They are all so kind and welcoming. I'm actually planning to go to a bar with a few of them in a few minutes. The bar we are going to is called "The Leaky Cauldron" and it's a Harry Potter theme! I know how much of a nerd you are Lucy"

"No way. I heard about that place on insta. I'm so jealous! Please take pictures and send them to me."

"Don't worry Luce, I'll send you lots. So what do you have going on during this fine Thursday night?"

I walk over to the kitchen and open the fridge, grabbing a bottle of sparkling rosé, I squish the phone in between my shoulder while I pop open the wine.

"Oh you know, just the usual. Vampire Diaries, some rosé and petting Rufus. Michelle texted me earlier and told me she's staying at a hotel closer to the firm because it's taking over her life. I can't wait until you're home. It's killing me to have to wait to watch the next episode of Grey's Anatomy without you. I might just watch it." I smile knowing the reaction I'm about to get.

"DON'T YOU DARE LUCY RAE WATERS. I will kill you if you watch the season finale without me"

"Hehe I know I'm just kidding. But I do really miss you." I take a sip of the rosé right from the bottle and slump against the counter.

"I know, me too. You need some more people in your life, you deserve that much. Hey! Earlier I was scrolling through twitter and I saw my friend just got a pen pal from prison. I know you're always trying to help other people. If you got a prison pen pal it would be a win win. You get to talk to someone who needs a friend, and you get another person in your life!"

I put the phone down on the counter and press the speaker. I reach up and grab a wine glass from the middle shelf of my cupboard and pour a glass of rose. Then I stick the cork in the bottle and place it in the fridge.

"Kiera, I don't know........"

"Just think about it, Luce. You aren't doing anything tonight anyway, just sign up!" I scowl at the phone.

"Hey! You're making me sound like I don't have a life!!!" I hear her laugh over the phone.

"Lucy, when was the last time you went out to a club? When was the last time you had sex since Kyle a year ago?"

"Yeah, Yeah I get it I get it. I'll sign up." I roll my eyes and sit back on the couch.

"Yay! Good girl Luce. Ok I got to run. Update me on who you get as a pen pal. Maybe it'll turn out to be a really fun girl and she will join our squad." I smile at that fun idea.

"Ok go go, send me pictures! Also, check in on your girlfriend, she seems swamped. I'll update you if I sign up. Love you!"

"Love you too Luce and will do, bye!" I hang up the phone and place it beside me. I reach over to the side table and pick up my silver Macbook Pro. Placing it on my lap, I pull up google chrome and type into the search engine "prisonpenpal.com". Immediately it comes up with a web page, and I click on the home screen. On the home page it shows pictures of inmates smiling with letters, and two girls, one in an orange jumpsuit and the other in jeans and a t-shirt hugging and smiling for the camera. I start to get excited. This could be a great way to meet a new friend! I also will feel like I am genuinely making a difference in their life.

I click on the button that says "sign up" and it comes up with a section where you put your information. I write in Lucy Waters, age 23, Pediatric Nurse, No criminal record. Then there is a section about hobbies and interests. I write, play piano, ukulele, read, play with Rufus, and like to paint occasionally. Then at the end of the document there is a place where you can add in a photo. I pull up my laptop's camera roll, and put in the photo that Kiera took of me at a bar. That was the first time I felt confident after Kyle broke up with me 2 months earlier. That was a rough time. Kyle and I had been best friends since sixth grade, and late high school, it turned into something more. I was crazy in love with him and thought he was my soulmate, until I walked in on him making out with a random brunette at a party. That shattered my heart, and it took me a few months to fully get over him. That photo of me sitting at the bar, drinking a martini in a sparkly silver cowl neck dress is my favorite photo of myself because it shows my inner strength. After I add the photo, I press submit. The webpage processes for a few seconds and displays a message that in a day or two I will be matched up with an inmate around the same age as me. I smile and take another sip of my wine. This is another step forward in trusting new people again.

Chapter 2

The next day I am sitting in the pediatric clinic break room, eating my lunch of a turkey and cheese sandwich when my email dings. I see it's from prisonpenpal.com, and I immediately smile. My finger presses on the app and I scroll down to the email. As soon as I click on it, a photo of the inmate I am paired with pops up. His piercing dark eyes instantly draw me in. They are framed with straight dark brown brows, and his cheekbones pop, making him have a deep contour and a sharp jawline. His hair is slightly wavy and it is in a thick tousled style on his head.

Braden Valencia.

My stomach bursts with butterflies, and I can feel my cheeks go a little pink. Wow, he is hot. I cannot believe I was paired with probably the hottest inmate in the history of inmates. What the hell am I going to write to him! I can't just write anything, he's too hot.

I take a deep breath. What am I thinking? He is probably a nice person that's lonely and needs a friend. It doesn't matter what I send him as long as it's from the heart. I look over at the clock on the wall and jolt out of my seat. Shit! I am five minutes late from my break. I pack my leftover lunch into my small bag and put it in the fridge. Then, I walk out of the break room and walk up to the front counter. Grabbing the clipboard of patients waiting, I read out the name of the child that's next and take them back. I'll worry about what I'm going to write to Braden later.

Later that day I am sitting at my kitchen counter, writing out what I am going to say to Braden. I had printed out his picture and put it next to my phono on the counter so the letter felt more intimate. At first it was challenging to write but after a few minutes I got into the groove.

Dear Braden,

Hello, my name is Lucy and I am your new pen pal. I have never done this before, nor do I know all the details of this program, so I will be learning as I go. A little bit about me, I am 23 years old and I am a pediatric nurse. I graduated from nursing school a year and a half ago and got a job at a clinic near my home in Seattle. So far, I really enjoy what I do. Kids are the funniest humans, and they make everyday fresh and exciting. I live with my puppy Rufus, who is the cutest german shepherd you will ever meet. He is my guard dog and my cuddle buddy all in one. I have attached a photo of him just in case you want to see his cute face. When I am not working, I like to hang out with my best friend Kiera and her girlfriend Michelle, play with Rufus, read my books, and I paint a little. Currently, Kiera is at a convention for women engineers in Atlanta so I am figuring out other things to do while she is away. Where are you located? Are you near Seattle or in another state? I don't know if they paired us up by location or just randomly. Anyway, what do you like to do? Also, what is prison like? I have never been in one or talked to anyone who has been, so I don't know anything more than what is shown on Orange is the New Black. I hope you have a good day Braden.

Talk to you soon,

Lucy :)

I place the letter and picture of Rufus in an envelope and lick it shut. Then, I tie my pink silk robe close to my body, slip on my fuzzy white slippers by the door and walk out of my apartment. At the end of the hall there is a mail shoot, so I place the letter in there. As I walk back into my apartment I wonder about Braden. I wonder how long he has been in prison? What if he did something really bad to be in there? Hopefully he is nice, I am just trying to make a new friend and hopefully help him out. I shake my hands trying to get all the anxiety out that is coursing through my body. After Kyle cheated on me, I found it really hard to meet and trust new people. Every time I would get close to a new person, I would pull away before they had the opportunity of hurting me. I am definitely getting better though as time goes on. I think that my job gets me out of my comfort skills, and it helps me face that fear of mine because I meet and talk to new patients everyday. It is still nerve racking though, opening up to a new person that I have never met.

I sit on the floor and pet Rufus's head. I still have a couple errands to do this Friday night. I need to go grocery shopping and since it's the first of the month I have to try to call my brother. Maybe I'll call him first and get it out of the way. I take out my phone, dial his number and wait a few seconds. Then, the sound of his familiar voicemail chimes through the phone. I speak the memorized words of the voicemail while it plays. My heart sinks a little, but at this point I am used to it. No use dwelling over a person who has made it plenty clear that he wants nothing to do with me. Next up tonight, grocery shopping.

I get up off the floor and walk into my bedroom. I take off the robe and slippers I'm wearing and slip on some mom jeans, a black turtleneck, and a white crew neck sweatshirt on top. I pull on my nike crew socks, put on my air forces, and turn the light off. I grab my black shoulder bag from the kitchen counter and lock the front door. On my way out I wave at the doorman Kenny. He is a teenage boy who works here during evenings to earn some extra cash. He is super friendly and is the best because he always makes sure that I am the first to receive packages and letters in the building. Trader Joe's is only a block away from my apartment complex and I am only buying enough food for half a week, so I don't need to bring my car and waste gas. Usually, I walk to the store in the daylight, but currently it is dusk.

As I enter Trader Joes, a few guys are smoking and leaning against the entrance. They turn to look at me, and immediately start whistling and calling me names. I roll my eyes and send them the scariest death glare I can manage. As soon as I send them my killer glare they stop laughing and try to disguise their giggling with coughing. Believe me, this situation is not new. Growing up in Seattle, I am used to guy's catcalling me or following me around simply because I am a woman. Around 16 I learned that if you send them a scary, killer look, they will stop going after you because you are no longer an easy target. But unfortunately that is not always the case.

In the grocery store I take out the list that I tucked in my purse and scan the isles for the items I need. I grab everything I need, pay at the register and walk my two bags of groceries home. I am excited to hear from Braden. I wonder when I will get a letter from him.

Chapter 3

After an eventful day of going to the farmers market, working out at the gym and taking Rufus to the vet for a checkup, I am finally back at my apartment to relax and enjoy my Saturday evening. On the way back from Rufus's vet appointment I stop by my mailbox. When Kenny comes out of the back room, he hands me a big yellow envelope. The handwriting that displays the address is extremely neat, and sharp. It reminds me of Times New Roman font. The return address says Washington State Department of Corrections. Interesting, so Braden is located in the same state as me. Rufus and I walk down the hall to my apartment, unlock the door, and plop down on the brown leather couch with Rufus's head on my lap. I tear open the neatly written envelope and pull out two sheets of paper and a few pictures. I am so excited that I immediately start reading the letter.

Lucy,

It is nice to hear from you. My name is Braden Valencia and I am 25 years old. I have never been assigned a pen pal in my year and ten months of being here, and I thought I would not be assigned one as I get released in two months. I am excited to get to communicate though, it has been a while since I have had outside contact. I think it is interesting that you are a pediatric nurse. Before I was arrested and convicted for a drug crime I had just graduated from business school. I am happy that you enjoy your career, just by reading your description of it, I can tell it brings you a lot of joy. As for the questions you asked me, I am located in the Washington State Correctional Facility. It is about two hours away from Seattle, where you are. I graduated from UW and lived in Seattle before my arrest, so I am familiar with the area. Your question about prison is funny. I suppose it is similar to Orange is the New Black, but a lot more real and unjust. Things here are not romanticized and shit can go down if you aren't careful. Your other question was about what I like to do. For me, it is challenging to have hobbies in prison, but I manage. I am a big bookworm. I saw that in your letter you said you also like to read. What is your preferred genre? I like classic books, like Jane Austen and Tolstoy, but occasionally I enjoy a thriller or science fiction work. Other than reading, I like to be active. I find that if I stay still for too long I get anxious. A few questions for you are how has your week been? Did you have any encounters with rude or dramatic patients you can share? I hope you didn't but I am sure sometimes kids can be a handful. Final question, tell me the story behind the photo you posted. You look happy but with another emotion I cannot put my finger on. I hope the rest of your day is great. I added a few more photos of me in the envelope, they are all I had to give to you. Also, please tell Rufus hello from Braden. He really is cute.

- Braden

I pick up the pictures that Braden sent and examine them. The first is a photo of him in a leather jacket with a chain and black ripped jeans. He is on UW campus and standing next to a statue of the mascot. I smile. He looks like he has a hard exterior but is a softie inside. The second photo is him sitting on his bed in what I'm guessing is his prison cell. He is wearing an orange jumpsuit and this tight around his arms and is cropped just at his ankles. His strong arms are covered in intricate tattoos that honestly look good on him. I wipe my lip just to make sure I am not drooling. Jesus Christ, I'm in trouble. I wonder what it would be like to run my fingers through his silky dark hair and feel those strong arms hold me close to his chest as he leans in and .... Lucy, oh my god chill. You got one letter from this man and are already fantasizing about him. I peek down at Rufus and see his adorable little head resting in his lap, but all I am thinking about is writing back to Braden. I can only imagine how excited Kiera is going to get about this.

****

Chapter 4

I waited until Sunday night to write Braden back because there is no post on Sunday so I had more time to write. Currently, I do not have a desk in my apartment and my kitchen counter is dirty from the pasta dinner I just made, so I am sitting on the piano bench with the cover over the piano. If my mother was around right now she'd kill me for using her precious piano as a desk, but there is no way I am writing this letter on the floor. Honestly, I haven't been able to play the piano since she passed. I took piano lessons from my mom for eight years, and won a ton of awards, but now I just cannot bring myself to play. It just feels wrong without her here.

I tap my sheets of notebook paper on the piano to straighten them out. I start to write.

Hi Braden,

So good to hear from you. I really enjoyed your letters and pictures. I put the pictures of you on the bulletin board that has photos of all my family, friends, and Rufus. My week has been pretty good, thank you for asking. Actually, work has been surprisingly busy. Right now, we are in the heart of flu season so there have been lots of appointments made. My guess is that this busy schedule will continue for a couple weeks, so I am mentally preparing myself. As for any crazy patient experiences, so far this week there has been none. Last week though was a whole different story. This one dad and his son came in because the son had the flu. I treated the son in the room, but the dad was staring at me the whole time. Kind of creepy if you ask me. Later that day when I was closing up the clinic for the night, the dad drove back to the clinic and tried to break in while I was cleaning some of the rooms.Thankfully, my coworker Ryan was there and called the police. Poor guy, I think he was just really high or something.

Anyway, that was my crazy patient experience for this month, hope you enjoyed it :) Usually though, my job is amazing. No complaints. It's cool to hear that you went to UW for college, I have a few coworkers that did pre-med there. The campus is so pretty, especially in the spring when all the cherry blossom trees bloom. I did not attend UW, but I did go to Seattle University for my nursing degree. To think about it, I am surprised we didn't run into each other. We were so close! Your other question was about that photo of me at the bar sipping a martini and smiling. That is my favorite photo because not only was I undeniably happy with my best friend Kiera being with me, but that was the first time I felt confident in myself after my boyfriend of four years cheated on me. That's probably the other emotion you are picking up in the photo.

Moving on, I think it is so cool that you like to read as well. I like to read mostly fantasy, romance, and sci-fi, but occasionally I read the classics. My favorite classic is To Kill a Mockingbird by Harper Lee. I have probably read that book at least twenty times. I am not sure if you have access to it where you are, so I'll send it to you. Please excuse the notes in the margins, I get a little excited about the story :) I hope you have a good week!

Talk to you soon,

Lucy

I walk into my laundry room that's on the side of the kitchen and pull out a yellow envelope from the bottom drawer. In my room, I walk up to my nightstand where my well-loved To Kill a Mockingbird is placed and I slip it into the envelope. Then I go back to the piano, fold the letter, put it in the envelope, close it, and address it to Brenden Valencia. In his letter he seems so…. Mysterious. I cannot place my finger on it.

He does not seem like a stereotypical drug addict that I have treated before in school. He has to have some sort of backstory. I know that this Harper Lee book is probably going to not matter to him, but it's important to me. It's really personal to give to him with all the notes in the margins, I still cannot believe I am sending it to him. But somewhere in my gut, I feel comfortable with him. A feeling that I have known him for a long time. On my way to take Rufus out for a night time walk, I drop it off to Kenny at the front desk.

Thankfully, Kiera gets back in town tomorrow so I will have someone to talk to about Braden. I should probably mentally prepare myself for all her screaming that is going to happen while I show her the letters. I giggle to myself. Kiera is so amazing, I am so lucky to have her as my best friend.

***

I am napping on the couch after a long day at the office when Kiera busts through the door streaming

"I'm home Lucy Goosey!"

I immediately spring up from the couch and tackle Kiera into a hug.

"I missed you so much Kiera! I am so happy you got home safe."

She squeezes me super tight and lets go. Kiera sets down her suitcase, takes my hand and drags me over to the couch.

"So Luce tell me everything! How was work? What about Braden? What's going on with him?" Kiera asks while squeezing my hand and smiling big.

"Umm, work has been fine, other than that weird break in fiasco nothing out of the ordinary has happened at the office. As for Braden" I suppress my blush and smile.

"He did reply to my last letter. And Kiera.... He's great."

Kiera breaks out into the biggest laugh and does a happy dance.

"Lucy is in LOVE with an inmate. Show me the letter! I need to know everything!"

I walk over to the piano to pick up Braden's letter and photos that I set there earlier. On my way back to the couch, Kiera snatches the items from my hand and plops back down on the couch. I watch her silently read the letter he wrote, occasionally looking up at me and wiggling her eyebrows. I sit down next to her and point to the picture of him sitting on his bed.

"Kiera just look at him, he is sooooo..."

I drift off at the end of the sentence because I get distracted by his strong forearms while he is leaning forward over his knees.

"Delicious. Girl. If I was not in a two year relationship with a woman, I would be jumping his bones. Speaking of, I should call Michelle, last time I talked to her she seemed stressed."

I nod.

"That sounds like a great idea, poor Michelle, the guy she is suing sounds like an absolute handful."

"Lucy, have you checked the mailbox yet, any new letters from Mr. Biceps?"

Kiera smiles at me and gets up to slip her shoes off.

"Oh no not yet! Let me go check with Kenny."

I leave the apartment and take the silver elevator down to the first floor. While approaching Kenny's desk I see his head is down across the desk and he is fast asleep. I lightly tap his arm.

"Good morning sleepyhead. I was wondering if there's any letters for me."

I giggle as Kenny shoots up and puts his hand over his chest.

"Jesus Christ Lucy! You scared me."

Kenny flips around in his chair and walks into the mailroom. He emerges back with a large orange folder.

"Here you go, sorry Lucy, if I knew it came I would have called you."

I smile and wish him a goodnight. Returning back to my apartment, I see that the letter is from Braden. Immediately I rip it open and plop back on the couch to devour his writing.

Lucy,

So good to hear from you again. I am so happy to hear that I made it onto your bulletin board, your photo is tucked safely into my diary. Also, I am so glad that you enjoy your job as a nurse. I don't know any nurses that went to Seattle University but I do know a few people that went to UW that are pre-med. Seattle University sounds like a great school though from what I've heard of it. As for the break in at your job, that sounds scary. I'm so glad you weren't hurt, people can be maniacs. Good thing Ryan was there, is he your boyfriend?

It's horrible to think that the photo you sent me was the first time you felt confident after your last relationship. I am sure that soon you will meet someone that is great for you if you haven't already met them. On another note, thank you for the copy of To Kill a Mockingbird you sent me. I love the book and I have really enjoyed getting to read your handwritten notes on the margins. They are so special. I also wanted to mention that I do have visiting hours on Saturdays from 8 am - 10 am. No pressure if you are not comfortable meeting, I definitely understand if it is too soon. Just an option. Can't wait to hear from you again, make sure to update me on any new books you are reading and any new shows you are watching.

- Braden

I take a deep breath to calm my butterflies. He seems so sweet and like he genuinely cares about my interests. Not even Kyle asked that many questions about me. I also did not miss how he sneakily asked if I had a boyfriend. Am I making this up or does he sound..... flirty. I mean, no complaints here. He seems very sweet. Before I know, I am grabbing paper from the printer, a pen from the kitchen, and plopping down on the piano bench to write my next letter to Braden.

***

Next week, Bradens POV!

Chapter 5

POV Braden

1 month. 30 days. 720 hours. 43200 seconds until I am released from Washington State Correctional Facility, and I am so excited. Prison has been rough. I never expected to end up here, but one thing led to another and here I am. At the beginning of my sentence I signed up for the pen pal program here, never expecting to be chosen because only one in fifty inmates get assigned one. Usually, they are people who have gone through the judicial system and know the unfairness that we experience everyday.

These pen pals are coveted by any inmate. To have the opportunity to make a friend that is outside these walls and are not weighed down by the heaviness of the system, it is a real treat. I never thought I would get one, until a month ago when I received a letter. I opened it up to find a note written by the most beautiful girl I had ever seen.

She wrote about her passion for nursing, her puppy Rufus, and her best friends and I couldn't get enough. Something about hearing a person be so excited and interested in something other than beating the line in the cafeteria and who is on guard tonight was a breath of fresh air. Being in here can be draining, but hearing her talk is so refreshing. The picture though was what got me.

Lucy was leaning against a bar with a martini and a shiny dress that clung to her curves in ways that made me feel small butterflies in my stomach. She has the most genuine and kind smile plastered on her face, and it made me remember that there's people out there that genuinely enjoy and live every moment of their life. Now, every time we get mail on Wednesday mornings I am the first one in line. Just hearing her talk about her work and her week were enough for me to push through this last month.

Maybe when I am out I can take her out to lunch. Will I even have enough money to afford that? That is another problem, with a criminal record, it will be challenging to find a job after I am released. I have just enough money to support myself for a month until I am broke. Hopefully I can find some sort of income before that happens. The programs for released inmates are horrible, they do not provide any sort of aid or transition back into outside life. I have a parole officer I have meetings with once a month, but that is it.

The last letter I sent to Lucy asked her if she wanted to come visit me here during my visiting hours. I would never expect her to come, but I had to ask. She is so smart, kind, and joyful, I would regret meeting her in person. I have another set of visiting hours, Mondays from 4-6, but that is when a few of the sex offenders have their visitation hours and I do not want them to have any eyes on Lucy. There have been instances where visitors are harassed by inmates during their hours, and I would kill them if they lay a hand on Lucy. Saturday's visiting hours, the ones I told to Lucy, are when most of the drug convicts have their hours. Most of them are spacey and wouldn't hurt a fly. I am near the end of my sentence and I am in good John, the guard who helps schedule visiting hours, so I have two available times.

It is Wednesday morning, mail day, so I line up by the door and wait for my letter from Lucy. I am excited to see how she responds to come meet me during my visitor hours. Most of me is expecting a no, but a sliver of my mind has hope.

"Hey brother, you waiting for that little lady's letter?"

Gerald Heptic, a convicted sex offender and overall creep slides down the stair railing and saunters over to me. I resist the urge to punch his brains out for talking about Lucy and instead settle on a death glare and a clenched fist. It's my fault that Gerald knows about her. We were crossing paths in the cafeteria, and the photo of her that was tucked into my diary fell onto the ground in front of him. After that day, he has had no shame about bringing her up every time he sees me.

"Gerald, I am not your brother. Leave. I'm just waiting for the mail like I do every week."

I turn my head away and try to ignore him.

"You're pretty lucky, ya know, I have 4 years left, maybe i'll be paired up with a girl that is that sexy as yours. Agh, it's too long to wait, maybe I'll just share yours, huh?"

Gerald says with a disgusting smirk on his lips. He knows he is angering me, and it is working. I turn around, grab him by the throat and shove him up the wall.

"Never talk about Lucy like that again. She is a kind person that does not deserve your disrespect."

I let go of him before any guards notice and he drops to the ground on his ass. I shake out my hand and give him another death stare. Before Gerald could get another word in, a guard slams the door open and brings in the mail. I walk over to the guard, tell him my name, and receive the letter addressed from Lucy. Her handwriting is so curvy and lovely, it's so interesting. Once I am back on my bed, I tear open the envelope and start to read her note.

Hi Braden,

Good to hear from you again. Receiving your letters is one of the best parts of my week! Speaking of this week, so many things have gone down. Kiera got a promotion, so we are celebrating this Friday by going to dinner at The Pink Door in downtown Seattle. Have you been? Michelle has been once on a work outing. She is a lawyer and told me that they have great live music. They apparently also have great ravioli! Not only that, but that weird guy that broke into the clinic a few weeks ago was sneaking around outside again. I called security and they are putting in an updated security system and more cameras. Thought you would want to know since you like to hear about all the workplace drama. I usually close the clinic with Ryan and he is trained in martial arts, so I feel safe. As for your question about Ryan, he is not my boyfriend, I do not have one at the moment. Honestly, I really haven't dated in a while, my last boyfriend left me heartbroken and I haven't had the chance to meet a lot of new people recently. On another note, I am so glad to hear you are enjoying my copy of To Kill A Mockingbird and that you like my little notes. Some of them are from middle school so hopefully they aren't too embarrassing. As for your visiting hours this Saturday, I would love to come. I have never been to a correctional facility before, so I don't really know what to expect! My shift at the clinic starts at 11 so I can only come for an hour, but I would really like to meet you. I will fill out the visitor form online by this weekend so I can come!

Great to hear from you again,

Lucy

Hearing her talk about her exciting week and how she cannot wait to go to The Pink Door, one of my favorite restaurants, is so cute. I wonder if she would wear that sparkly cowl neck dress that she has on in the photo. The way it hugged her breasts and was cut at her upper thigh would make any man fall to his knees, including me. If I ever see her in that dress, it will be hard to keep my hands to myself. Just the thought of slowly pushing the hem of that sparkly dress up her thighs and sucking on the exposed parts of her breasts against the wall is enough to make me have to adjust myself on my bed.

Lucy writing about that man creeping around the clinic made me feel worried. Men can be dangerous in this world, and I'm sure some of them would easily target Lucy in her pink work scrubs and her genuine smile. It calms me to know that they are putting in a new security system, and that Ryan knows martial arts. It calms me even more to hear that she is not dating anyone right now. Whoever that guy was that broke her heart, I will go after him if he ever tries to hurt Lucy again. Her letter surprised me the most when she said she was coming to visit me this Saturday. I wonder what she will be like in person. Will she be quiet? Super outgoing? Nervous? Beautiful? I take a deep breath. I cannot wait for this Saturday.

Hope you all had a good week!

Chapter 6

Lucy's POV

The sun shines through my window as my alarm rings loudly and wakes me up. Stretching my arms over my head, I kick my legs out from under my comfy sheets and plant them on the floor. Today is the day I meet Braden. My stomach feels slightly twisty and my heart races at the idea that I will be coming face to face with him. I've never been to a prison before, hopefully this visit goes smoothly. I did have to sign a consent form online before I could sign up to meet Braden, and that was nerve racking. It listed multiple things that could go wrong during the visit, including harassment, being held hostage, or violent threats. I had to sign my signature right under. It makes me wonder, am I doing the right thing? Braden seems like such a perfect gentleman in all of his letters but what if something happens during our visit. I asked Kiera if she would be willing to come with me, but she had to tour a job site for her work right when I would meet Braden.

I think everything will be okay.

I take three long and deep breaths before I start getting ready for the day.

Walking into my bathroom, I brush my teeth and clean hair, put on some everyday makeup, and swipe on deodorant. As for my clothes, I decide to wear a pair of dark wash mom jeans, a crewneck sweatshirt and an oversized tee shirt on top. I accessorize with a small silver chain and two small silver rings on my left middle and right ring fingers. Changing into my scrubs at work is the best option for today as they have printed on them the name of my clinic, and I am not sure I want anyone to know where to find me. I am sure nothing would happen, but just to be safe, I fold and tuck my light blue scrubs into my tote bag. The clock reads 7:00 am, which is perfect because it takes about 45 minutes to get there. I throw my tote over my shoulder, slip on my white Nikes, grab my work water bottle, and head out the door while yelling bye to Rufus on my way out. Kiera usually feeds him breakfast because she leaves before me, and then the stinker goes back to bed to sleep off that big helping of food. Even though he is only 3, Rufus acts like a cute little old man.

On my way to the correctional facility, I drive through Starbucks to get an iced caramel macchiato and a croissant for breakfast. This is an occasional treat I allow myself if I am on the road and do not have time for breakfast. I consider picking something up for Braden but remember that I am not allowed to bring food items in without them being searched/ sniffed. Just to avoid that, I choose not to bring him anything. Sorry Braden, you'll just have to survive another month without Starbucks.

Finally, I pull up to the facility. It does not look as scary as I would expect. The boxy building is a faded yellow color and windows line each of the sides. The building is set on top of a grassy hill and has metal gates lining the perimeter of the lot. On each corner is a small watch tower.

I pull up to the silver metal gates topped with barbed wire and press a button on the pin pad that says "get ticket here". The kiosk dispenses a small white ticket and the gate buzzes open slowly. An officer in a little outdoor cubicle by the gate nods at me and looks back to their computer.

Pulling into a parking spot, I place the ticket on my dash, grab my tote, and walk into the lobby. Walking up to the front desk, I notice there is a small waiting area to my right, and a door to my left that has two officers in front and a large metal detection device that you walk through at the airport.

"Hello Ma'am, are you here to visit?"

A male officer at the front desk looks up at me and squints.

"Uhhh yes yes. I am here to see Braden Valencia. I filled out all the papers online and signed up to see him at 8 am."

I fumble around with the strap of my tote bag, nervous while the officers click through tabs on the computer. He searches for a few minutes while clicking his tongue in the most annoying and condescending way possible.

"Aha, found ya Miss Waters. Looks like you filled out all the required paperwork online. Now I will have you step over to your left and go through security. He squints at me weirdly.

"Don't want you bringin anything in that don't belong."

I awkwardly smile and look to my left.

"Thanks."

When I approach the two guards outside the door, they tell me to set down my purse on the little table to my left so one of them can quickly search it. Then the other female officer tells me to slowly walk under the metal detector. After a few seconds of no beeping, the officer opens the door and gestures at me through. I grab my bag and follow her down a hallway.

"Is this your first time visiting?"

The officer asks me as we walk together down the white walled and brown floored hallway.

"Yes. I have never been to a correctional facility before. I am just here to visit my penpal that I was assigned through the program offered here."

She smiles.

"That is so kind of you to sign up to be a penpal. I know a few inmates that have pen pals and I can't tell you how happy they are to receive letters. On the schedule it says you are visiting Braden. He is very nice, never causes any problems."

I blush and sigh. That's a relief. At least I know now that Braden is not a troublemaker. I don't know how I would act around someone that is rude or insensitive. I never got the vibe that he was any of those things in his letters, so I am not shocked he is nice in real life.

"That's great to hear. I got the feeling that he was a great person from reading his letters every week."

The officer turns a corner to the right and we continue walking.

"He always listens to me when I talk about my kids and my crazy Italian husband. He even tries to offer insight on why my husband is acting the way he does. I know it can be hard here to get along with the correctional officers, and I can see why. Some of us are assholes. That guy at the front desk, Rick, is a jerk. Watch out for him. But I think Braden sees that I took this job because it was the most high paying job I could get with no degree in this area. I'm just here to support my family, not to get on anyone, and Braden is cool for respecting me. I think he also knows that I am the first one to support any new programs for inmates and any new reforms to this messed up system."

She takes a deep breath and smiles at me.

"Sorry for blabbing, I am just so excited that Braden has finally got a visitor. He hasn't had one since the beginning of his sentence."

She stops in front of a silver door and pulls out a key to insert into the hole.

"No, I liked hearing about him. It makes me less nervous to meet him."

The officer pushes open the door and gestures for me to walk through it.

"By the way, I'm Cynthia. Nice to meet you."

I shake her outstretched hand and look up at her.

"I'm Lucy. It was also nice to meet you Cynthia."

Cynthia nods her head, wishes me luck, and tells me she will come back for me at 9 am. As she leaves the room I wave goodbye to her. She was nice and honestly hearing her talk so highly of Braden makes a calming feeling wash over me. That does not last long because as soon as I turn around from waving goodbye to Cynthia, I am met with two pairs of piercing dark eyes from across the room.

My eyes flicker down and take in his form. His figure is large, and muscly, but not bulky. His orange jumpsuit clings to his strong biceps like glue as he slightly leans over the metal table he is sitting at in the corner of the concrete covered room. I can see some minimal black tattoos brushing his skin from underneath his collar and his right forearm. My eyes look back up to his face and I observe a sharp jawline and chiseled cheekbones that pop. His black hair is mussed atop his head, slightly curly and certainly soft. I wonder what it would feel like to grate my hands through those shiny curls. I am sure it would feel like heaven. Why does it feel like there is no oxygen in here?

I quickly remember that I am still staring at him, like a lunatic, and snap out of it. I clear my throat and carefully walk over to the silver metal table. He does not take his eyes off of me. I stand right in front of Braden and gingerly reach out my hand.

"Hi. I am Lucy. It's nice to meet you."

Braden slowly gets out of his sitting position and rises to his full height, towering over me at 6'4. The height difference of a whole foot makes my knees weak as I look up to meet his eyes. He is standing just close enough that I can slightly smell his scent of morning coffee and some sort of spice. It wraps me up and makes me want to take a step closer to him. Braden delicately takes my outstretched hand and shakes it. As soon as our hands touch I blush and look away for a second.

"Nice to meet you Lucy, I'm Braden."

I slightly freeze as his smooth voice came out of his mouth. It is deep and smooth, but has a slight grit to it at the end of his words. I take a slow swallow and sit down on the metal bench connected to the table because the burning tension is getting higher and higher.

"So, is it what you expected?"

Braden asks while he rests his hands on the table and slightly leans towards me. I look down and notice his wrists are handcuffed together. A rush of heat travels right down to my core as I imagine those on me, in a different context. I immediately clear my throat and look back up to his eyes.

"What?"

Braden smiles.

"The prison. Is it what you expected it to look like?"

I unwrinkle my eyebrows and give him a small smile back.

"Sure. I mean I did not expect it to be this light and spacious, but I could see how movies and TV exaggerate the space."

"Nobody gave you trouble though, right? When you came in?"

He looks straight into my eyes and looks at me with a slightly concerned expression.

"No, no. For the most part everyone was nice. Cynthia especially, I really like her."

Braden furrows his dark eyebrows.

"What do you mean for the most part? Did something happen?"

He repositions in his seat to be more angled toward me. I also notice that he subtly starts to scan the room with an intense look.

"It really wasn't that big of a deal. I just got a weird vibe from Rick at the front desk but that's it."

Braden sighs and sits up straighter. He takes his hands that are tied together and lightly brushes through his thick dark locks.

"Yeah. Rick is rude sometimes. Let me know if he gives you any more trouble and I will take care of it."

I blush, exhale, and look down. He's already trying to protect me and he hasn't even known me for more than a few weeks. I wonder what he is like with the other people in his life, and if he is even more of an alpha male.

"Hey, speaking of Cynthia, she mentioned that I was your first guest in months. Do you not like the company? We can totally just talk in letters if you prefer."

My heart sank at the suggestion, but I would do whatever was most comfortable for him.

"Oh no! I love the company, it truly means so much you came."

Braden squeezes my hand that I have resting on the table and my stomach fills with butterflies.

"Honestly, I don't have a lot of people to come and visit me. I am an orphan and my only friends I had were the ones that I took the fall for. We all would sell illegal drugs to make some extra money and when we got caught, they threw me under the bus. I could have fought for less time but honestly, they had families and I didn't. I know it's messed up but I knew I could handle it."

He looks down while telling his story, avoiding eye contact. I am surprised. I was not expecting him to be so open about his past, but here we are. I feel important and trusted, which is not a common feeling I have with men.

"Wow. Thank you so much for sharing about your past with me Braden. I am so sorry that you had to take the fall. That sucks. I know I can't really relate but I lost my parents too, so I somewhat understand what it's like to be on your own. But your journey has been more challenging. I guess I want to let you know that I would never judge you for anything in your past."

Braden looks deeply into my eyes as I give him back a small hand squeeze.

"Thank you Lucy."

He continues to look deeply into my eyes, but now with an emotion that I can't quite put my finger on.

"Anyways, you mentioned you get released sometime soon? When is the date?"

I try to steer the conversation to something a little more lighthearted.

"I get released in about a month. I am very excited, I have even started to pull some photos down that I have hanging on the wall in preparation."

"Exciting! Do you have a plan for what you are going to do after?"

I ask him while crossing my legs and leaning my chin on my hand that is propped up on the table.

"Not yet. I know I have to stay close to this area because I have monthly meetings with my parole officer, but other than that I have no plan. Hopefully I will find a job after this. I have a business administration degree from UW that I got on scholarship, but it's hard to imagine getting a job in the corporate world now."

I sigh and feel bad. It sucks that even after he has done his time and grown as a person that people still won't hire him. He would be such a great employee with his caring attitude and his bachelor's degree.

"If I run into anyone that's hiring I will put a good word in for you."

Braden smiles cheekily.

"Thanks Lucy, that would mean a lot. So, do you have any fun plans for this weekend? I think I will just be re-reading your cute margin notes that you wrote in the To Kill A Mockingbird book you sent me."

I giggle and blush at his fun weekend activity.

"I am glad you like the little notes. I think tomorrow night Kiera, Michelle, and I will be going out to celebrate Michelle's win on her lawsuit. Michelle is Kiera's girlfriend and she has been spending all her time dealing with this case. I just found out she won it so we will be celebrating."

While I am talking, Braden subtly brushes his eyes down my long legs that are shown off in these tight jeans. His eyes darken slightly and he flicks his tongue over his bottom lip, wetting it slightly. Something else might also be getting wet slightly. I pretend not to notice and continue talking to him unwaveringly. The only sign that I caught him checking me out is the tinge of pink blooming over my cheeks.

Braden and I continue sharing about our lives, and he asks me about the Vampire Diaries, how Rufus is doing, if the creepy man at my work has come back, and if Kiera and I have done anything fun recently. I love how he remembers all the little details of my life and is excited to ask about him. He has this tough and brooding outside but really, he is such a teddy bear. I get so sucked into our conversation that it feels like it's only been five minutes when Cynthia comes back to walk me out.

"You ready hun?"

Cynthia asks as she approaches the table.

"Wow. That went by fast. Hopefully next time I visit I won't have work so I can stay longer."

I stand up from the metal table and brush my hands over my oversized tee to get out any wrinkles.

"It did go by so fast. I hope you can come by next Saturday too. Lucy, I really enjoyed talking to you. It's been a long time since I've looked forward to something until you came along."

I majorly blush and tuck a piece of my hair behind my ear at that comment. It also does not help my blush when Braden sweeps me into his arms for an amazing smelling hug. He has to lift both wrists over my head and bring his arms down around me because of the handcuffs, but I don't mind this at all. It happens to bring me closer to his chest.

"I will see you next week Braden, can't wait!"

With that, I step back from his hold and slowly turn and walk toward the door with Cynthia. Right before I leave the room I look back at Braden and notice that he has not taken his eyes off me. I immediately blush and continue out of the room.

Chapter 7

Sitting on the plush leather seat of the crowded restaurant and bar in downtown Seattle, I explain to Kiera and Michelle about my visit with Braden yesterday morning.

"Guys, it was honestly great. I felt so many butterflies it was crazy."

Kiera does a little squeal while Michelle, leaning back on her chair, gives me a smirk and a nod.

"I remember that feeling when I first met Kiera. You just know at that moment that you have met someone special."

Michelle leans forward, looks deeply into Kiera's eyes and gives her hand a firm squeeze. The two have been dating since the end of Kiera and I's college graduation. Kiera and I had gone out to a bar after graduation, ran into each other in the bathroom, and chatted all night long, leaving me awkwardly in the corner of the bar sipping martinis and escaping smolders from obviously taken men. I didn't mind though. Kiera deserves to be with someone as caring as Michelle. It also helps that Michelle is four years older than us. She keeps Kiera grounded while Kiera keeps her spontaneous. They have the kind of love that is unconditional.

"Ugh stop encouraging my overthinking! I have literally been replaying our conversation in my head over and over since yesterday."

I throw both my hands to my temples and try to rub the thoughts about Braden out of my mind. I've met him once, why am I going psycho!

"You got it bad huh."

Kiera observes and giggles. Michelle leans over, plants a small kiss on Kiera's neck, and closes her eyes while staying in her embrace. Kiera turns toward her and runs her hand through her box braids, moving them to the other side of Michelle's neck. I take that as my cue to give them a few minutes of privacy. They would never make out in front of me or make me feel un-included on purpose, but I know at this moment they really want some alone time.

"I am going to get another drink from the bar. Anyone want anything else?"

Both Michelle and Kiera turn to look at me and shake their heads no. Michelle gives me a grateful smirk and pulls Kiera closer. I stand up, brush the wrinkles out of my one shoulder, body con dress and walk over to the bar in the corner of the room. I plop down on another black leather bar stool and look over the extensive array of alcohol bottles that grace the wall in front of me.

"I'll have a long island iced tea please. Open tab."

The bartender nods at me, types a few things into an iPad, and starts to make my drink.

"Luce?"

A familiar voice calls my name and my spine immediately tenses up. The last time I heard that voice was a year ago over the phone, begging me to forgive him. Slowly, I turn towards him.

Standing right next to me, in all his glory, is Kyle Shaw, frat boy, douce, and my ex-boyfriend. He is dressed in a light blue button up tucked into khakis. His stupid, long, bleach blonde surfer looking hair is hanging loosely down the side of his head. The thing that infuriates me most though is the biggest, happiest smile spread right across his face.

"Is that really you Luce? Wow, it's nice to see you!"

Kyle props down in the empty barstool next to me and lays his elbow on the bar. Just as he sits down, my long island is set in front of me. I reach for the drink and Glug. Glug. Glug. I chug the whole entire long island in seconds. Between every glug I can see Kyle's smile drop more and more out of the corner of my eye. I aggressively set my drink back down on the bar and sigh.

"So I am guessing you aren't excited to see me?"

I turn my face toward him sharply and give him the dirtiest look I can muster.

"Stop talking to me. I can't believe you even have the audacity to talk to me after what happened."

Kyle looks stunned and rubs his thumb across his bottom lip.

"Ohp so we're going there, alright. Look Lucy, I just saw you and I wanted to say hi. It's been a whole year since I've talked to you and I have grown a lot as a person."

I look him up and down with a judgey look.

"You look the same."

He smiles and giggles.

"There she is, my sassy Lucy!"

I frown.

"I'm not your anything. At least I was until you decided to cheat on me after, what, four years? Stop acting like you are the victim when I was the one brokenhearted."

I look away from him and order a vodka soda from the bartender that asks if I want something else. Kyle turns towards the bar, takes a deep breath, and fidgets with his fingers.

"You're right Lucy. I messed up. I sucked. I don't even know what happened that night. I was waiting for you to get to the party and then all of a sudden I am making out with another girl. For the past year I have been beating myself up about it everyday."

I turn to smile at him.

"As you should be. That killed me, seeing you with that girl."

Kyle looks deep into my eyes.

"Lucy, I'm sorry. A lot has happened this year that put things into perspective and made me grow as a person. By coming up to you, I am really not asking for another chance. I just want to be able to talk to you again. I've known you since middle school, and it's weird for me not to know what's going on in your life. I know it's my fault it is this way, so I want to make sure that it isn't also my fault that I haven't reached out. Please, just let me be a little bit in your life again."

He looks genuine. I'm surprised. I have known him for years, so I can easily know when he is being truthful or not.

"What put things into perspective this year?"

I ask, wanting to know if he has anything to back his words up. Kyle leans back in his chair and runs his hand through his blonde locks.

"Umm Sherrie was diagnosed with breast cancer about a month after we broke up."

Wow. My heart skips a beat as what he says sinks in. I really like his mom, Sherrie. She was always kind to me.

"I'm sorry. Is she going through chemo? How bad is it?"

Out of habit, I slightly lean in towards him.

"It was stage two, so not the worst, but cancer is horrible, so it felt like the end of the world. The doctors were really worried about radiation not working fully so they decided to have her go through eight weeks of chemo. She did really well, and she finished cancer free earlier this year."

I smile and hesitantly nod. I am so thankful that Sherrie is okay.

"Through all of that I have realized what is most important in my life. I regretted all through her treatment what I did to you because having you there for support would have been amazing."

I sigh. Cancer sucks and it does have a huge effect on people when they or a loved one go through it. Maybe he has changed a bit.

"Wow Kyle. That's a lot. Are you doing okay now?"

"Yeah, I feel healed and ready to move forward. Again Lucy, I am not asking to get back together right now. I just want you in my life again."

Honestly, would having Kyle back in my life again be that bad? He seems a little different now, and resenting him might cause me more stress than letting him back in. I look into his eyes and mumble,

"Okay."

Kyle's face morphs into a huge smile and he pats my shoulder gently.

"Thank you."

He says gratefully.

"I am going to get back to Kiera and Michelle but, see you around?"

I slip the bartender my card, sign the receipt, and slide off the stool. Kyle pulls me in for a side hug and I return it.

"Sounds great. Get home safe Lucy."

***

After explaining the whole entire conversation to a heated Kiera ready to pummel Kyle, I finally get her to calm down in our apartment lobby.

"Lucy, I know he seems different but do you remember how hurt you were. Michelle and I sure as hell remember. You were crying on the couch watching Pitch Perfect on repeat for weeks. Half my paycheck was going to buy you ice cream!"

Kiera says loudly while stamping her foot. The echo can be heard from all the way across the spacious lobby.

"I remember that! Lucy, that time was rough."

Kenny chimes in from behind his desk. His job was pretty simple so he was always looking to eavesdrop on anything interesting.

"Guys look. I am not planning on letting him back in fully. I am just done wasting brainpower on resenting him."

Kenny raises his eyebrow at me and gives me an incredulous look.

"Oh, butt out Kenny. I am sure you have better things to do than listen to my life drama."

I sassily remark as I lean over his black polished desk.

"Actually, no I don't. This job is so boring. I am so happy I am not working here for much longer."

Kenny bends down to pick up his fallen magazine as he gives us time to let what he just said sink in. Michelle, Kiera, and I all yell at the same time.

"WHAT?!"

"What do you mean you're not working here for much longer? Are you leaving?"

I sputter out as fast as I can manage.

"Yeah, did I not tell you guys? I got into the zoology program at Oregon State! I am going to college in a few weeks!"

I immediately smile and lean over the desk to give him a hug. Ever since Kenny started working here, all he would talk about was his love for wildlife. I am so proud.

"Who's taking your spot as the doorman?"

Michelle asks out of curiosity as she leans one elbow on the desk.

"I am not sure yet. The owner of the building is on vacation for the next three months so he said I was in charge of hiring and training someone new. I haven't started looking for someone else yet. Do you know anyone that wants an all paid apartment and a job sorting letters all day?"

My eyes burst out of their seams. Before I can stop myself I respond.

"Yes. My friend Braden is looking for a job and an apartment!"

Immediately Kiera and Michelle whip their heads to me and drop their jaws.

"Lucy! What if he is a psychopath getting out of prison! You don't even know him yet!"

Kira throws at me while Michelle puts her hand on my shoulder. I think about it. It would be a perfect opportunity for him.

"Kiera! He is such a nice person. He only got convicted for a drug crime. You have done hard drugs before so who are you to talk! And are you forgetting what your girlfriend does as a career? One wrong move by him and Michelle could have him behind bars in a heartbeat."

Michelle shrugs and looks at Kiera.

"Kiera, she's right. Inmates that committed drug crimes are usually harmless when they get out if they don't have an addiction."

Kiera pinches her nose and turns to look at Kenny.

"Oh so now you're quiet Kenny-boy?"

Kenny looks between us and cracks a smirk.

"Look guys, if he has working hands and is willing to start in a few weeks, it would be a good fit."

I smile. Kiera rolls her eyes.

"Oh, she knows he has working hands."

Kiera whispers in my ear and I smack her arm.

"Next time I see him I will let him know about the job."

Kenny gives me a thumbs up and reaches to answer the ringing phone. Imagine, Braden living and working in the same apartment building as me. I could see him everyday. He could come over to my apartment, watch movies, cuddle, chat about our day, have his hand rest on my thigh. Lean into his alluring embrace whenever I want to. That sounds amazing.

I can't get ahead of myself though. He could easily say no. I would understand, he has only met me once and I offer him a job. I hope he doesn't see it as charity. I just want to make him happy because I care.

Sorry for no update last week, I was on vacation with no WIFI! Hope you enjoyed the chapter!

Chapter 8

I find myself, again, walking down the white hallways of Washington State Correctional Facility with Cynthia.

"So, Lucy, how did the last visit go? Was it awkward meeting Braden for the first time?"

Cynthia asks as she walks to the visitor room where I will meet Braden for the second time.

"It was great! He really is nice. I feel bad though, I wish I would have known him sooner so he would have had more visits."

I got paired up with Braden basically two months before his release. It is only my second visit and he gets released in three weeks on parole. If only I signed up for a pen pal earlier I could have offered him more support.

"It's alright sweetie, I am sure he is grateful for any time with a pen pal, even if it is just a few visits."

Cynthia keeps putting her hand over the pocket of her black slacks where her phone is placed. With her shoulders tensed and her eyebrows slightly raised, it looks like she is anxiously expecting a call.

"Everything okay Cynthia?"

Breaking out of her trance, she quickly tears her hand away from her pocket and flips her head to look at me.

"Yes, sorry. I- well, my husband Lorenzo got into a small car accident this week. He feels fine, but the doctor wanted him to go in today to have a checkup. He is very stubborn and won't admit that he feels off, but when he sits down or stands up he scrunches up his face like he is in pain. I am just anxious to hear what the doctor reports."

Cynthia smiles grimly and looks down to the floor, trying to avoid eye contact. I feel horrible, I hope her husband is alright. Hopefully Cynthia gets good news from the doctor soon.

"Oh my god, I am so sorry! Please, don't feel bad checking your phone while I am here. Really, I don't care. I hope everything turns out okay."

Cynthia looks back up at me and gives me a quick hug.

"Thank you Lucy."

The two of us keep walking until we reach the visitor room, where Cynthia leaves me at the door. Turning around, I make eye contact with Braden's dark eyes from across the room and move towards him.

"Hey, good to see you."

Braden says and stands up to put his cuffed hands over my head to bring me into a tight hug. I deeply inhale his amazing scent and snuggle closer into the hug. He chuckles and I feel the vibrations across my chest. We pull away and sit down at the circular metal table together.

"How are you today?"

I ask while taking my phone out of the back pocket of my pants and stashing it in my white purse.

"I am doing pretty good. Nothing super eventful until you got here."

I smile.

"Me too. Thankfully, I don't have to work today, it's my day off. Work has been kicking my ass. I have been working non-stop 12 hour shifts for the past 4 days."

Braden's eyes bulge and he reaches for my hand.

"Wow, I am glad you have today to rest. Do you have any plans for today other than sleeping?"

I tell him about how I just started watching a new series called Love Island, and how I got Michelle interested in watching it with me. I am sure that tonight we will be enjoying at least two episodes while Kiera joins us only for the wine. We continue talking, and it feels so comfortable. I feel like I can open up about anything in my life and he won't judge. I don't even know if I felt this comfortable with Kyle who I've known most of my life.

Throughout our conversation, Braden makes a conscious effort to touch me in little ways. When he laughs at a stupid joke I made, he rests his hand on my arm for a second or two. I also get small butterflies when our feet brush against each other under the table. All I want is to reach over and cuddle with him but I know I can't.

"Oh my gosh, I almost forgot. My friend Kenny, who works at the front desk of my apartment building, just got into a zoology program and will be heading to college in a few weeks. He is looking for someone to fill his position, and in exchange receive a salary and an apartment. I might have mentioned to him that you were interested, and he gave me a flyer with all the information."

Braden drops the hand that was resting on my arm and stares incredulously into my eyes.

"I know I totally overstepped and I didn't ask permission but I just thought-"

He interrupts me by shaking his head and giving me a huge smile.

"Are you kidding me Lucy! That would be a dream. A job, a salary, and an apartment. That would be amazing."

I immediately sigh of relief. I hoped he would react like this and not get defensive or angry.

"But, I don't think I'll get it. I am sure Kenny has other applicants, and as soon as he sees my record he won't even bother to follow up with me."

Braden lays his head in his hands and shakes it from side to side looking stressed.

"Hey, hey, it's okay. I already told Kenny that you will be released and on parole. He seemed fine with it and not even phased."

Braden looks up at me from his hands and his shoulders relax.

"Kenny is just trying to find someone to fill his spot as soon as possible. My guess is he wants to move down to Oregon State a little early to get some party action."

He smiles at me and shakes his head again.

"You are awesome. I can't believe you got me an opportunity to get a job and an apartment. Am I dreaming right now?"

Braden continues to be excited throughout the rest of our visit as I see him periodically glance down and re-read the flyer that I brought him from Kenny. It's cute how appreciative he is. People visiting around us start to get up and leave, so I look down at my watch. Visiting hours are over and I hear Cynthia coming to get me.

"Braden, want to walk with us? I'll drop you at your cell after we walk Lucy to the lobby."

Cynthia offers while I stand up and grab my purse. Braden smiles and stands up with me. All three of us walk together out of the visitor room and down the hallway. Braden notices Cynthia's anxious behavior today and decides to mention it.

"Woah, Cynthia. Are you okay today?"

Braden stops her in the middle of the hallway and rests one of his strong large hands on her shoulder.

"Yes, sorry. Lorenzo got into an accident and I am just waiting for the doctors to call."

Just as Cynthia explains herself, her phone buzzes. Her eyes snap wide open and she immediately reaches for her phone located in her pocket.

"You don't mind if I get this? It will only take a minute, or I-I can drop you off first and listen to the voicemail? Its, It's really not a big-"

Braden interrupts her by shaking his head.

"Take it Cynthia, we will just wait here."

Cynthia sighs gratefully and answers the call while running into the break-room a few doors down. I realize this is the first time Braden and I have been alone, unmonitored. It feels exhilarating and I start to feel a small heartbeat in the pit of my stomach. The air feels electric.

"Poor Cynthia. That family has been through a lot."

I nod to agree with him and turn to face him.

"So when I get back to my apartment, should I tell Kenny that you will take the job. Do you need more time to consider? I totally understand if you do. I mean it's weird that a random girl comes to visit you and offers you a job and you don't really know-"

Braden stops my word vomit by stepping close to me and placing a warm thumb over my mumbling lips. The touch makes my heart skip a beat.

"No, I would love to take the job. It is perfect. I get a salary, an apartment, and"

His eyes darken as he runs his thumb downwards so that my bottom lip curls. He lustfully licks his lips.

"I get to see you."

I immediately blush and look down.

"I would like that. A lot."

We get interrupted by harsh footsteps stomping down the hall towards the two of us.

"Hey! What is going on over here!"

Rick stomps down the hallway, a furious look plastered across his face as he places one of his hands over the part of his belt that is holding his gun. Startled, I instinctively take a step into Braden's embrace. His solid arm curls around my middle and brings me to his side.

"Where is your guard Braden? Give her to me. Let go of the visitor."

Rick's face is scrunched up in a dangerous expression while he reaches out, grabs my arm, and jerks me from Braden's side.

"Don't you touch her. Step away Rick."

Braden steps in between Rick and I and removes his hand forcefully from my arm. I cower behind Braden's large frame and cling to the fabric of his jumpsuit.

"Where is your guard! You aren't allowed to be on your own!"

Rick yells while popping open the carrier of his gun. Braden slowly takes a few steps back and presses us into the wall. His strong, warm body is laying flat against me as he protectively places a hand on my hip behind him.

"Rick, calm down."

"HEY HEY HEY. Rick put that gun away. I am right here."

Cynthia comes running out of the break room and scolds Rick while taking out her walkie talkie from her belt.

"Rick, if you don't calm down, I will have to call for backup. I was grabbing something from the break room and I was only gone for a few minutes."

Cynthia steps in front of Braden and I and lays a firm hand on Rick's chest. Rick takes a minute to cool down, looks between Braden and I multiple times, and backs down the hall where he came from. As he is walking backwards he points at Braden.

"I'm watching you bitch."

Braden clutches his fist and tightens his jaw. I reach out, take his clenched fist in mine, and brush my thumb over his fingers. He immediately relaxes and takes a deep breath.

"What the hell was that? Did Rick just come out of nowhere?"

Cynthia asks as she rubs her forehead. I step out from behind Braden and stand next to him.

"Pretty much."

"Hey, Cynthia, how was the call?"

I ask, trying to move the conversation away from the scary situation that just happened. My heart is still beating fast from it and I would prefer to have a distraction.

"Oh, all good. Lorenzo has a slight concussion so he needs to hydrate and rest, but other than that he is healthy."

"That's great Cynthia."

Braden says and gives her a small smile. I can tell he is still pissed but is trying to hold it in for Cynthia.

"Okay, you two ready to go?"

I nod my head and follow Cynthia and Braden to the lobby doors, the same ones Rick disappeared into a few minutes prior.

"When you walk by him don't make eye contact."

Braden says as he wraps me up in a big hug and squeezes me tightly.

"Ok, I will. Bye Braden, see you next week?"

He nods and Cynthia and him watch me walk through the lobby doors with a concerned look on their faces. While I walk through the lobby, I look down towards my shoes and quickly walk through the exit doors.

I could feel Rick's eyes burning into me every step.

Chapter 9

He leans down and captures my lips into a searing kiss. He hums husky in my ear as he pins me up roughly against his cell wall. My fingers rake the back of his orange jumpsuit, feeling the strong muscles move under the breathable fabric. He moves his lips to my neck and slowly places wet kisses in a downward motion. I pull at the front of his jumpsuit, impatiently undoing the buttons and lifting up the white muscle tank that is lying below.

Braden chuckles as he wraps my legs around his waist and grinds into me at a slow but sensual pace. I run my hands through his hair and direct his mouth toward my hard nipples that are pushing against the fabric of my tank top. Braden swiftly grabs the bottom of my top, pulls it off of me, and latches onto my pebbled nipple. I breathlessly moan as I feel my panties moisten and a knot in my stomach start to form. I tug at the bottom of his jumpsuit with need.

"Off. I need these off."

I whisper breathlessly into his ear. Braden immediately pulls me off the wall and lays me down on top of his bed. He -----

"Lucy!! Wake up! The party starts in half an hour and you aren't even dressed yet"

I moan and slowly stumble out of bed and smack the light switch on. Woah that was quite a dream. Tonight is Kenny's going away party and I have been up since six am picking up flowers, prepping food, cleaning the apartment, and trying to vacuum every piece of Rufus's hair from the couch. I got home from getting some last minute decorations at two, and I immediately fell asleep in my bed. Now I have half an hour until the party starts at seven and I am still in sweatpants.

Standing in front of my closet, I consider what outfit to go with. Michelle is wearing a blazer and Kiera is wearing a cocktail dress, so definitely something on the fancy side. Digging through my drawers, I decide to wear a sparkly navy blue mini dress that hugs my hips nicely.

As I comb through my hair and touch up my makeup, I can't help but feel bad for Braden. His visiting hours were today but I wasn't able to see him as I was crazy busy with the party. Thankfully, Cynthia was able to get him ten minutes of phone privileges tonight at eight so I can talk to him. I am very excited. I wish he could be here at the party. Maybe soon.

Knock, Knock, Knock.

It looks like the first guests are here! We decided to invite some of our neighbors, friends, and coworkers to the party. Even if all of them don't know Kenny, the people we invited will make sure the party is fun.

I fluff my hair one more time and walk into the kitchen where Kenny, and our friends Bruno, Justin, and Clint just arrived. I greet them all with hugs and serve everyone drinks. A few minutes and a few arrivals later, the apartment is packed with lots of friends. I am busy refilling the chips and dip when I feel someone place their hands on my hips and give me a hug from behind. Surprised, I flip around and take a few steps back from my ex Kyle.

"Hey, sorry you scared me."

I greet while awkwardly rubbing my arm. It felt strange to have him touch me intimately like that. We haven't been intimate for a whole year, and him touching me like that brings up memories.

"Oh sorry for scaring you, you looked busy filling up the appetizers. How are you doing Lucy?"

Kyle says as he takes a few steps into me. I take a deep breath and try not to be awkward.

"I have been doing well, just working and hanging out with friends. How is your work?"

Kyle leans back against the fridge and blatantly checks me out from head to toe. I avoid eye contact and take a sip of my wine.

"It has been going well. I've been at Facebook now for two years and I really like it. What friends?"

Kyle asks while eating some chips and dip.

"What?"

"You said you were hanging out with friends. What friends Lucy?"

"Oh well, I signed up to be a prison pen pal a while ago and I have been visiting my friend Braden who is currently in prison. He is super nice and I really enjoy visiting him."

Kyle stops eating his snack and looks up at me in a jealous manner.

"Isn't the point of a pen pal to write letters and not visit them? That's kinda weird Lucy that you visit him. What if he is dangerous?"

He says while showing worry and squeezing the hand I have sitting on the counter. I take my hand out of his and cross my arms defensively.

"Kyle, he is very nice. We got along so well in the letters that he invited me to his visiting hours. And anyways, he will be released in a week so it's not like he hasn't served his time."

Kyle chuckles and leans back against the fridge again in an arrogant manner.

"Good luck to him finding a job with that record of his."

I smirk.

"Actually, he is taking Kenny's job when he leaves for college. It's a perfect fit. He gets a salary, an apartment here, and a job."

Kyle scrunches up his face in annoyance.

"Great, so I guess he will be around a lot."

"Yes! I am so excited, you have to meet him! I think you would like him, Kyle. And to be friends again, we have to be friends with people that are important to each other."

He sighs and rolls his eyes.

"Fine, I'll meet him. But only if you go try that new sushi restaurant that just opened with me."

I squeal with excitement. I think the wine is kicking in.

"Fin's Sushi? Yes! I totally want to try that!"

Kyle smiles and we continue talking about sushi until Kiera reminds me that it is 5 minutes to 8pm and I have to call Braden. Kyle looks a little angry when I walk to my room but I am used to it. When we were in a relationship, he was always very possessive. I would talk to another boy and he would threaten them, especially if he had alcohol in his system. Honestly, it started becoming scary and was one of the main reasons I was able to get over him.

Once I am in my room, I dial the name of the facility and tell the operator that I want to speak to Braden Valencia. As the phone rings, I finish my third glass of wine and set it down on the nightstand.

"Lucy. Hello."

Braden greets in his rich warm voice that sends shivers down my spine.

"Braden! So so good to hear your voice! Sorry I was not able to visit today, I was crazy busy prepping for Kenny's party."

I collapse back on my bed and fiddle with the jewelry that is hanging around my neck.

"It's ok, I am getting to talk to you now. Speaking of, how is it going? It seems rowdy from what I can hear."

Braden chuckles.

"Yes, it is very loud and it's hard to get around out there. I swear I've tripped at least four times tonight. I hope Kenny likes his party. I wish you were here."

It might have been the wine or the butterflies in my stomach but I let that last part slip out.

"Hey, I will be there on Friday."

I smile and get excited. Wow, that's so soon. I wonder what it will be like to see him here, in my world.

"I am excited. Hey I was going to ask, do you need a ride here? I work on Friday from 12 pm - 8 pm, but can I pick you up before or after?"

"No, no don't worry about it Luce, I can find a ride there. There is a bus route that goes right in front of the facility, so I'll just take that."

I get the tingles in my cheeks and I blush at his nickname for me. Ok the wine is definitely kicking in.

"I like that."

"What"

He almost whispers with a deep rasp. I swear I can hear him run his big hands through the soft locks of his hair.

"The nickname you just gave me. It's cute, just like you."

I slur the end a little bit and Braden chuckles through the phone.

"Okay, I think you have had a little to drink. I don't want to keep you from having fun. Go enjoy the party and I will see you Friday night? Or Saturday?"

He is so cute how his voice gets higher when he gets excited.

"Yes! I will be tired and possibly smelly after work but I would like to see you!"

"Sounds great Lucy. Be safe tonight and drink lots of water! I will see you in a week."

I blush and cuddle the pillow that is next to me. Ugh I wish he was this pillow.

"See you soon Braden."

Even when the line goes dead, I keep the phone pressed up against my ear, trying to grasp onto the feeling of being and talking with him. He is a rush of serotonin that makes me forget to think. I feel immersed in a feeling of being cared for, and I like it.

Sure, Kiera and Michelle have my back but when was the last time I was taken care of instead of caring for someone else? It has been a while, and even him checking in on me made me feel warm.

The rest of the night is a blur. After I lost at Kings Cup for the second time, I don't see anything except slow motion memories. I have never been this drunk, and I have been drinking since I was sixteen.

Something didn't feel right.

My head feels heavy while my body feels like a bowl of noodles. Next thing I know, I am being pulled into my bedroom by my wrist and embraced by a man. I don't catch his face as he aggressively pushes me backwards onto my unmade bed. Suddenly, I know what is happening, but it's like I can't understand the situation. Everything is fuzzy and there is a ringing in my ears. I get enough mental effort together to push the body off me and tell them to get out. I think I was loud enough because he quickly leaves the room and I collapse back on the bed. All I can remember is staring at the wall with a pit in my stomach and Kiera and Michelle shaking me. After that, my mind goes dark.

Chapter 10

The warm light filters through the white curtains hanging in front of my window signaling to me that it is morning. I slowly rub my eyes, and look around my space. I am still dressed in my navy blue mini dress, I have lipstick smudged all over my face, and my bed sheets are strewn all over the floor. I suddenly remember last night's events and my mind goes numb.

What the fuck almost happened last night. I was obviously drunk and that person tried to take advantage of me? Why does every memory from last night seem so groggy? Is it possible I was drugged? A million questions pop up in my brain as I strip out of my dress and wash myself in the shower. I only had a few glasses of wine and two white claws after losing the drinking game. How could I have been so out of it?

I step out of the shower, dress in comfortable clothes and walk out into the kitchen where Michelle and Kiera are standing around the counter sipping coffee. Immediately when I enter the kitchen they put their coffees down and Kiera brings me into a huge hug.

"Lucy, are you doing okay?"

Michelle asks while looking across the island at me in a concerned way.

"Yeah, I just feel really groggy and I don't remember specifically what happened last night. It's weird because I didn't drink enough to black out."

I respond and hug Kiera back. I put on a brave face because Michelle and Kiera can get really protective. I move away from Kiera and grab a glass from behind where Michelle is standing. Grabbing the cold brew from the fridge, I fill up the glass with coffee, ice, and creamer.

"Lucy, why did you scream? Michelle and I heard a loud scream from your room, we ran in, saw you laying on your bed with lipstick smeared everywhere, and then you passed out. Did something happen?"

Kiera narrows her eyes at me knowing I will probably avoid the question. I surprise her and tell them both the truth.

"I really can't remember too much. I was drinking out here with everyone and then I was dragged into my room and kissed aggressively. He was too strong to push off of me so I screamed and he left. I passed out right after."

"Oh my god. Lucy, I can't believe that happened. I am so sorry."

Kiera takes my hand in hers and I squeeze it. Michelle steps forward with an angry look and slams her hand on the counter.

"I swear to god Lucy I will kill whoever touched you in court. Do you remember anything about them? Could it have possibly been Kyle? I will file a report as soon as I get to my office. Whoever this was is going down in flames."

My stomach drops and my eyes widen. I don't want to talk about this anymore. It's so scary to think someone that I trust enough to let into my apartment would have tried to sexually assault me. I don't even remember what they look like, and if I file a report they would just get angry. They might hurt me. I can't bring Michelle and Kiera into this.

"No no, I don't want to take legal action. I-I want to stop talking about this, I can hardly remember details from last night."

I bend over the counter and take some deep breaths as I start to feel overwhelmed. Michelle places her hand on my back and gently gives me a few pats.

"Lucy, it wouldn't be a big deal, just a statement and -"

"No! I don't want to talk about this anymore."

I interrupt Michelle and try to calm myself down. Flashbacks from last night start to come into my mind and I don't want to think about them. I'm okay, I'm safe now. Kiera narrows her eyes at me.

"Look Luce, I can tell you are overwhelmed right now so I will back off, but if you remember anything about who it was that tried to assault you, you need to tell us."

Michelle places a hand on Kiera's arm to calm her down, but looks at me and nods in agreement. I realize that they aren't going to drop this until I agree, so I make eye contact with both of them and shake my head yes. Both of them take a deep breath and we disperse, starting to make our usual breakfasts of avocado toast and scrambled eggs.

I can tell Michelle wants to say more but doesn't want to overwhelm me, so breakfast is mostly quiet other than us talking about our plans for the day. I work at twelve, so I change into lilac scrubs, throw my half dried hair into a ponytail and head out the door while yelling bye to Rufus, Michelle and Kiera.

It is now Friday night, Braden's first night training/working, and I am headed home from my shift at the clinic. Even though it is 8pm, I hope he hasn't eaten because I am picking up tacos from the truck near my apartment. Wow, I guess I have to say our apartment complex now. I get butterflies just thinking about him standing at the front desk, flipping through letters with his strong fingers, dressed in anything other than that bright orange jumpsuit.

I am only five minutes away from the complex when I suddenly realize my hair is a mess, I have the bare minimum makeup on, and my pink scrubs have random stains all over it. At a red light, I reach over to my glovebox and pull out my little emergency kit. Unzipping it, I layer on some deodorant, spray some light perfume, and pop in a stick of gum. By the time the light changes to green, I am at least less smelly. Well, I guess this is a preview of what Braden will see in the mornings when I come down to grab my mail in my unicorn pajamas.

Pulling into my parking spot, I get out of my car, grab my work bag, the tacos, and walk into the lobby. Right away, I see Braden hunched over, digging through a mail bin while Kenny reads off a list he holds in his hands. As soon as I walk in though, the two look up at me and I make eye contact with Braden. It blows my breath away just to see him here.

He is dressed in a tight fitted black tee, black ripped jeans that show off his strong thighs, and a silver chain necklace. Not to mention his hands are covered in a few silver rings that make my heart skip a beat. Before I know it I am walking over to Braden and standing right in front of him. We don't talk for a few seconds, we just look into each other's eyes and take in this electric and breathless moment.

"Hey Lucy! Good to catch you, it's my last day and then I am handing over the job to this guy!"

Kenny interrupts with an excited smirk, obviously not understanding that Braden and I were having a moment. I snap out of my trace and turn to smile at Kenny.

"Kenny, I am so excited for you! You have been talking about this program for so long, I am sure you will do great!"

Kenny grins and digs around in a bin for something specific.

"Oh Lucy, this is my last time giving you your cosmo magazine. We have to soak in the moment!"

Kenny says as he hands me the magazine. I giggle.

"For sure. How is everything going? Training going well?"

I turn to look at Braden and notice that he is already looking at me. I blush a little and look around.

"It's going great. Pretty simple procedures, I think I will have it by the end of my shift today."

I smile at Braden and hold up the tacos I bought.

"What time do you get off? I bought these tacos and Michelle and Kiera won't be home until late because they have an outing for Kiera's job. Want some tacos?"

"Sounds great Lucy, I get off in about ten minutes."

I could be wrong, but did Braden just blush? A light pink color washes over the tops of his cheekbones and my stomach fills with butterflies.

"Uhhh where are my tacos Lucy? You can't just forget about me!"

Kenny jokingly asks while winking at me. I lean over the counter and swat his elbow.

"Ok Braden, want to meet me at mine, I'm apartment number 312!"

He nods his head with a warm smile. I wave at both of them, wish Kenny good luck at college and make my way to the elevator. I travel up three floors, walk into my apartment, drop all my things on the floor of my bedroom, and run into the bathroom.

Quickly, I strip out of my scrubs, throw them into my hamper, and step into a pair of grey joggers and a matching crop top. Then, I brush out my hair, put on some chapstick, and brush my teeth. As soon as I am done brushing, I hear the doorbell chime and Rufus bark. He's here.

I walk over to the door, take hold of the gold knob and pull. There he is, leaning sexily against the doorframe with his arms crossed, showing off his hard muscles. I gulp.

"Hey, come on in."

I open up the door wider and he strides in, looking around.

"I like all your decorations Lucy, it's definitely you. And is this Rufus?"

Braden bends down to pet Rufus who has rushed over and is now rubbing up against him, asking for cuddles. I giggle and bend down to pet Rufus too.

"This is! He is so happy to finally meet you."

After a few seconds of cuddles, Rufus walks over to his dog bed and lays down for a nap. He is the kind of dog that likes attention for a little bit, but is very independent.

"I hope you are hungry, I picked up the best tacos in town!"

I walk over to the island to start unpacking the bag and Braden sits on a barstool next to me. As I am laying out the tacos, he reaches up and pulls gently on the ends of my long loose hair. I giggle, brush his hand away, and go and fill up some water glasses from the fridge.

"Do you want any hot sauces? I think I have tapatio and sriracha somewhere in here."

Braden gets off the stool and comes up behind me to help look for the hot sauce that I can't seem to find in the fridge. I blush instantly when he lightly presses up against me, innocently helping me look. Nice move Braden.

"Ah ha! Here is some tapatio."

Braden reaches over me, grabs the hot sauce, and places it on the counter.

"Ok, I got two chicken tacos and two beef tacos. Want one of each or do you prefer a flavor?"

I plop down on one of the barstools and Braden follows, sitting next to me. He brushes

one of his thighs against mine and a shiver runs down my spine.

"I'll have whatever you don't want."

He says. I lay out one of each type of taco for him and we dig in. He eats the tacos really

fast and I feel bad. Hopefully he isn't still hungry.

"Braden, are you still hungry? You ate that really fast. I could make you a grilled cheese, or a turkey sandwich, or a -"

He smiles and cuts off my babbling by squeezing my upper thigh. Heat races to my core and I swallow.

"No, I am good. Those were the best tacos I've had in forever. Thank you Lucy."

I smile and nod. After finishing most of my tacos, I wrap up my leftovers and place them in the fridge while Braden throws away our trash that is sitting on the counter. Once we have cleaned everything up, I ask if he wants to watch something together. He excitedly agrees and we plop down on the couch together.

Reaching behind us, Braden pulls a blanket down and lays it across both of our laps. I thank him while I flick through the movie options on Netflix. We both decided to watch the new season of Outer Banks that just came out. Apparently, this was one of his favorite shows while incarcerated.

A few minutes into the first episode, apparently Braden does not like how far apart we are sitting because he snakes his arm around my waist, grabs my thigh and brings me into his chest.

I giggle at the not-so-subtle move, and snuggle into him, resting my head over his chest. I can hear the strong thump of his heartbeat under my ear and it slowly relaxes me. I feel like I am falling asleep until the hand Braden has resting on my thigh slowly moves a little higher. My stomach flips. A few seconds later it moves a few inches higher towards my core.

I bite my lip and try to keep my eyes locked on the screen. Just as I think he is done moving, I feel the brush of his soft lips behind my ear. Immediately, I bite my lip to look at him.

We make eye contact, and I see his eyes darken with a look of hot desire. He licks his lips while his eyes scan over my face, and rest on my lips.

Reaching up with his other hand, he tangles his fingers in my hair behind the nape of my neck and slowly, slowly inches closer to me, keeping his eyes locked on my lips. I take a deep breath, start to close my eyes and--

"Lucy! We're home!"

Kiera and Michelle bust through the door and Braden and I immediately break apart to opposite ends of the couch.

Chapter 11

Michelle and Kiera stand in the kitchen shocked as Braden and I awkwardly stand up from the couch and clear our throats.

"Oh hey! Um, I thought you guys would be home later!"

I say while I tuck a piece of hair behind my ear. By the way Kiera is smirking at me, I can tell my face is bright red.

"Lucy, it is later, it is 11:30."

My eyes bug out and I look over at the clock. Wow, it's already so late. Time really does fly by when I am with Braden.

"Is this the famous Braden?"

Michelle steps forward to shake Braden's hand. I roll my eyes at her when she puts on her intimidating face and squeezes his hand tightly.

"Yes, I'm Braden. I am assuming you are Michelle, and you are Kiera?"

Braden stops shaking Michelle's hand, puts both his hands in the pockets of his black jeans, and nods his head in greeting at Kiera. I go to stand next to Braden and loop both my arms around his right arm that has a space for me because his hands are in his pockets. As soon as I make contact with him, he visibly relaxes, making me feel warm and wanted inside.

"Yes, nice to meet you Braden. I hope you guys had a nice night....sure looked like you did based on the position you were in when we entered."

Kiera taunts while plastering on a shit-eating grin and wiggling her eyebrows at me. Immediately I blush and pull Braden to the door.

"On that note, we are going to go say goodnight."

I can tell Braden enjoyed Kiera's banter because as we were walking to the door he laughs and waves at the two of them.

"Nice to meet you guys! Have a nice night."

Once the two of us make it to the opened door, Braden turns around and takes a step closer to me. After a couple of seconds of gazing into my eyes, he brings his hand up to my cheek and gently caresses it.

"I really enjoyed tonight."

He mumbles, getting lost in the moment.

"Me, too. Hopefully we can see each other soon."

Nodding, Braden reaches into his pocket and grabs his phone. He opens up the contacts app and asks me to type my number in. My face breaks out in a grin and I quickly fill out my name and phone number.

"I'll text you my work schedule for this week, and we can figure out another night to see each other. This time, my treat."

"That sounds great, Braden. I think I don't have as many hours this week so we will definitely be able to do something."

He nods and pulls me into a tight hug. We stay in that embrace for a few seconds, just relishing in the feeling of being with each other. Pulling away, Braden places a light kiss on my cheek that leaves tingles all over my face.

"Goodnight Lucy."

"Goodnight Braden."

I wave at him while he walks down the hallway, eventually disappearing into the elevator.

A few days later, I am sitting in the break room of the clinic eating my salad and scrolling through my phone.

Unknown Number: Hi Lucy, this is Braden.

Butterflies creep into my stomach and I immediately text back.

Me: Hey! How are you doing?

Braden: I am doing great, just doing some grocery shopping. What are you up to?

Me: I am currently on break at work. Only a few more hours left of my shift!

Braden: I want to take you out tonight.

My heart skips a beat and I can't help but blush. I haven't been asked out by anyone in at least a year.

Me: I get off work at 7 pm. Is that too late?

Braden: No, how far away is your work from the apartment?

Me: Just about 15 minutes.

Braden: Let's go see that new horror movie that came out last Friday. I think I can get us tickets to an 8:00 showing.

I never watch horror movies because I am a scaredy cat and get nightmares for at least a week after, but with Braden beside me, I think I will be just fine.

Me: That sounds great. I'll text you when I am back at my apartment.

Braden: See you soon Luce.

Seeing that my break is over, I pack up my empty tupperware, fill up my water bottle, and walk back into the office to check in with one of our head pediatricians.

A few hours pass and when it is time to head home, my stomach is filled with nerves. A million questions run through my head. What if this date is awkward? What if he decides that I am weird or not worth it? What if I get into a relationship with him and he cheats on me again? Is this even a date? He didn't say it was a date.

When I get into my car to drive home, I take a minute to myself. Resting my delicate head on the steering wheel, I take a few deep breaths and remind myself that I can't just stay locked up in my apartment. I need to get out there and live up my twenties. Why not take this opportunity to go out, especially since it is with someone who literally makes my cooch light on fire when i'm around him.

After taking a deep breath and talking myself out of a hole, I feel a little better. I start the car, turn on the street, and head to my apartment. When I unlock my apartment I immediately go to Kiera's room and open the door.

"AHHHHHH"

I scream and slap my hand over my eyes. Michelle is butt ass naked straddling a half naked Kiera. As soon as I walk in and scream they dive under the covers.

"WHAT THE FUCK LUCY I THOUGHT YOU WERE AT WORK"

Kiera yells at me out of embarrassment. I try to walk out of the room but bang my head against the door because my hand is still slapped over my eyes.

"Ouch! I was just trying to borrow your zebra stripe pants! I have a date - well I don't know if it's a date - with Braden! Are you covered yet?"

They both assure me they are covered so I turn around and retract my hand from my eyes.

"Kiera I really need those pants, they would go so well with my leather blazer and they make my ass look really good."

Kiera sighs and rubs her temples.

"Fine, they are hanging up in my closet. Hurry, I was literally so close!"

Kiera complains. I grab the pants that are hanging and run out of the room.

"Gross, Kiera TMI!"

"Good luck!"

Michelle yells while I close their door and run into my room. Immediately, I strip out of my dirty work scrubs and pull on the zebra pants, a black crop top, my leather blazer, and my black Doc Martens. Entering the bathroom, I brush my teeth, and put on some deodorant. As soon as I am dressed, I shoot Braden a text saying that I am ready and asking if I should meet him at his apartment. He reads the text, but does not respond. Hmm. A few seconds later I hear a knock at the front door.

I open it to find a sexy Braden waiting on the other side of the door. He is dressed in a leather jacket, white tee, and ripped black jeans.

"Lucy, you look great."

Braden looks me up and down slowly, lingering on where my breasts peek out from the top of my crop top. He licks his lips and runs his hand through his luscious black locks. I smile.

"Thank you. You don't look so bad yourself."

I grab my black shoulder bag, close the door and lock it. As I am focusing on locking the bolt, Braden kisses my cheek from behind, lightly pressing his body up against the back of mine. Giggling at his suave move, I grab his hand and pull him down the hallway to the elevators.

"So, are you a horror movie fan?"

I ask Braden, leaning against the elevator wall.

"Yes. Something about rooting for your favorite characters and the suspense of not knowing if they are going to make it is so entertaining. Other shows just lose my attention."

"Hmmm"

I say.

"I am not the biggest horror fan. I watched Jaws one time and had nightmares for a week. Usually, I stick to romance or comedies."

Braden furrows his brows and takes a step toward me.

"Lucy, if I knew you didn't like horror movies I would have picked something different!"

"No, Braden, it's ok! I actually feel okay watching a horror movie as long as you are there next to me. Y-you make me feel safe."

When I realize what I just admitted to him, I turn bright red and look down avoiding eye contact. He brings his hand under my chin and moves my head upward so we make eye contact.

"Good. I will always be there."

Both of us exit the elevator, hop into my car and arrive at the theatre in time to make the 8 pm showing. I offer to Venmo Braden for the tickets but he brushes me off and refuses. When we make it into the theatre, we find that our seats are in the middle of the theatre, sandwiched between a couple that is currently messily making out and a man who looks like he has an olympic gold medal in weightlifting. Together, we sit down and get comfortable, or at least try to get comfortable because the huge thigh of the man sitting next to me is taking up almost all of the legroom. Braden notices, puts up the armrest between us, grabs my legs with his strong hands, and places them on his lap. He leans into me to ask,

"Is this ok?"

I nod reassuringly and rest my head against his shoulder. As soon as the movie starts, I scoot in closer to Braden. Every time a jump-scare would pop up on screen, I would turn my face into his chest and scream out with the rest of the audience. I think Braden was enjoying it though, because every time I would jump, he would gently brush his hand through my hair and laugh a little bit. By the end of the movie though, I was actually enjoying the storyline because the two main characters end up falling in love.

As soon as the lights come on in the theatre, I slowly untangle myself from Braden's arms and stretch my stiff arms above my head, yawning.

"Are you tired?"

Braden asks as we exit the theatre, his warm hand holding mine tightly.

"A little but if I go home straight away I will not be able to sleep."

He chuckles and asks if I want to go on a little walk by the lake that the cinema is located on. I happily agree.

"So, then you didn't like the movie?"

Braden asks nervously. I squeeze his hand reassuringly and shake my head.

"No actually, I really enjoyed it. Obviously, the jump scares weren't my favorite"

He chuckles and I lightly slap his chest, rolling my eyes.

"But, the storyline was great... and, I might have liked the cuddles."

Braden and I stop at the lake viewpoint, he wraps his arm around my middle and brings me into him. One thing I have noticed about Braden is that he always likes to have me in close proximity. If I walk across to the other side of the room, he will follow, or even if I am sitting a little bit away from him, he will bring me closer. These little actions bring butterflies to my stomach.

"Me too."

He whispers into my ear. Shivers run down my spine and I let out a breath I have been holding. I watch it cloud up around us in the chilly night air.

"So, now that you are living on your own, have you thought about contacting anyone from before you were incarcerated? Any old friends you have been talking to or checking up on?"

I ask out of curiosity. Braden sighs.

"There is one friend I have, his name is Clide and he is a chef at a steakhouse about twenty minutes from here. I just found him on instagram and I have been thinking about reaching out to him, but I haven't decided if I want to have any connections with people from my past. As for anyone else I knew before, no."

I nod and run my hand up and down his back gently.

"If Clide was a good friend to you and you miss him, I would encourage you to at least check in with him. But, it's whatever you're comfortable with. I will support you either way."

"Thanks Lucy."

Braden slightly smiles at me and I recognize gratitude in his eyes.

"Let's go back now, it's pretty cold."

While we are walking to the car Braden offers me his leather jacket multiple times, but I refuse, telling him that I am not going to have him catch a cold.

Once we are in the car and I am pulling out of the parking lot, I give Braden AUX power, which he happily accepts. While Braden pulls up one of his favorite artists, Phoebe Bridgers, he rests his palm on my thigh, immediately causing warmth to spread all throughout my lower body.

Entering the complex, Braden is tightly holding my hand, almost as if he wants to squeeze out all the sparks and tingles we feel when we touch each other, and save it until the next time we see each other.

Walking out of the elevator to my apartment Braden has scooched closer and closer to me. Now he is walking right next to me and I couldn't be happier. Pretty soon we arrive to my door and I turn to face him.

"Thanks for tonight. I truly had the best time."

"Of course, I really enjoyed seeing you, hopefully you aren't too scared of anything tonight. If anything freaks you out, give me a call and I will come running."

I bring Braden into a warm hug, wrapping my hands around his shoulders and embracing him tightly. His large hands snake around my waist and lift me up, my feet dangling off the floor for a few seconds. Laughing, Braden sets me down and looks deeply into my eyes. Sizzling tension fills the air as he slowly, gently, runs his finger through the back of my hair. Closing my eyes, I wait patiently for him to close the distance between us and place his soft lips on mine.

"Goodnight Lucy."

Braden takes his hands away from me, and swiftly walks down the hallway without a second glance. I am still standing outside my door looking at the empty elevators when it registers that he didn't kiss me. Without his hands caressing my hair and his body pressed up against mine, I feel cold and alone.

Why didn't he kiss me? Did I really just misread that whole entire date and conversation? Did I do something?

Disappointed, I unlock my front door and step into my dark and now creepy apartment. Remind me again why I agreed to watch that horror movie again? Oh yeah, because hot Braden asks me to go with him and all sense of myself flies out the window for a boy that obviously doesn't even like me?

I sigh loudly, rub in between my eyes, and walk into my bathroom. I am already changed into my unicorn pajamas, have all my makeup off, and my hair up in a messy bun when I hear a banging on the front door.

Braden's POV:

As soon as I make it to the door of my apartment I know I have made a mistake. More than anything, I want to kiss Lucy and feel her body against mine. But, as soon as I saw her there waiting for me to kiss me like an absolute angel, my doubts creeped in. She is a pediatric nurse. I am an ex-convict. There is no way I deserve her, I cannot drag her into my messed up life.

How can I not be with her though? We have such a perfect connection, she is breathtaking, and one of the kindest people I have ever met. I will never be good enough for her, but I am going to spend everyday trying to be. Starting now.

Turning around, I sprint into the elevator and press level three. I anxiously wait for the elevator to ascend, my mind filling with lust as I imagine her pressed up against me, moaning, and running her hands through my hair.

Before I know it, I am standing in front of her door, hurriedly banging on the door like my life depends on it. A few seconds pass by, and a startled Lucy opens the door slowly and peeks out.

She is dressed in baggy unicorn pajamas, a messy bun, and has acne cream placed on her forehead. She is perfect.

I reach out, take hold of her arm, bring her towards me, slam the door, push her smaller body against it, and reach down to connect our lips. At first she is surprised, but after a few seconds her lips melt against mine. Her lips are soft and her movements are gentle against my passionate and dominant ones. I wrap my arms around her inviting waist, bringing her closer and closer. I swipe my tongue against her lower lip asking for entrance. She immediately accepts and opens for me, sighing. I dive in, caressing her tongue with my own as I reach down and kneed her alluring ass that feels so good under my hands.

She tangles her fingers in my hair, pulling on the strands slightly, causing a growl to escape me. I push her harder into the door, making sure one of my hands is behind her head to protect her from any hurt.

With my other hand, I grasp one of her legs and pull it upwards so I can push against her fully, my hardness slightly rubbing against her core. I roll my hips slowly against hers which causes her to release a moan at my movements and pull back to relish in the feeling. I move my lips down, placing open mouthed kisses on her neck and down on the tops of her breasts. I reach up and massage her left breast as I lean down and suck on the top of the right one, enjoying the feel of them under my hands. I know if we keep going, I will end up fucking her against this door. I don't want anyone else to see her like this, so I decide to pull back and continue this another day when we have more privacy. I release her lips from mine, connect our foreheads, and stare into her eyes. We take a few breaths together, trying to regain the breath that both of us just lost. After a few seconds, I release her leg and breast from my hands and instead bring her into a loving hug.

"I just had to."

I breathe out just before I place a gentle kiss on her forehead.

"Well, it was a good move."

Lucy laughs a little and pulls back from our breathless embrace.

"You know what I just realized."

Lucy says with an annoyed grin on her face.

"What?"

"Braden, you just locked me out of my apartment."

Hope you enjoyed the longer update today!

Chapter 12

After knocking on the door loudly for a few minutes, a grumbling Kiera opens the door for me. Braden makes sure I make it inside safely and presses a swift kiss on my lips before heading back to his apartment. Laying in bed, I reminisce on our wonderful evening. That kiss. I haven't felt that amount of chemistry with someone ever. Every time I am around him, my heart feels like it wants to explode. I swear that I can still feel the whisper of his arms wrapping around me and his member grinding against my core.

The vibration of my phone draws me out of my daydreaming, and I reach for it.

Kyle: What are you doing tomorrow?

I swallow. I am still uncomfortable with Kyle's new presence in my life, how can I know he won't hurt me again? I can never know that fully, but he was in my life for so many years and he only broke my heart once. Does one bad action outweigh all the good that we had together? I know that I definitely don't want to get back with him. Once a cheater, always a cheater. Not to mention, I'm thinking about Braden 24/7. But being occasional friends? I could manage that.

Me: I have to run some errands in the morning, but I am free after 3 pm.

Kyle: Would you like to meet at that new sushi place?

I take a deep breath.

Me: Sure, what time?

A few minutes pass and Kyle responds.

Kyle: I just made reservations for Fin's Sushi at 6. See you there?

Me: Sounds great. Text me when you leave?

Kyle: Ok, I'll text you tomorrow. Goodnight Lucy,

Me: Night.

I am proud of myself. I am starting to trust people again. Maybe things will go well tomorrow and Kyle and I can rekindle our friendship.

The next day, after unpacking all the groceries I bought at Trader Joe's, I relax on the couch with some TV. While catching up on Vampire Diaries, I decide to check in with Kyle.

Me: Are we still on tonight at 6?

One episode of Vampire Diaries later, Kyle hasn't responded. Nerves start to form in my stomach, but it's only been a half hour so I ignore it. An hour passes and I decide to start getting ready for dinner. While pulling on a flowy sundress, I look at my phone. It is 5:00 and no response from Kyle. I text him again. Maybe he is napping?

5:15 and still no response. My stomach drops and my face gets hot. Did he forget? We just talked about this dinner. Maybe I got the date wrong? Pulling up the messages, I realize that I definitely did not get the time wrong.

I drop the phone on the counter and sit down on my bed deflated. I am so stupid. Why did I trust him again? Obviously he is just going to hurt me again.

Blurrrbbbbbb. My stomach grumbles.

I am starving. I forgot to eat lunch because I was out, and by the time I got home it was too late to eat something. I look down. My cute sundress and curled hair is smoothed perfectly, just waiting for dinner.

Deep breath. I am going to go to this dinner without him. I have a reservation anyways, and I was so excited to go. Even though Kyle let me down, I won't let myself down.

Grabbing my purse, I head down to the elevator, press the first floor button, and smooth my dress out while it descends. I catch a glimpse of myself in the mirror of the elevator. A disappointed feeling spreads through my chest. Is there something wrong with me? Why would he invite me out and then just ditch me?

These thoughts invade my mind so heavily that I don't realize someone is standing in my path through the lobby. Startled, I crash into the strong back of a person, the force knocking me back onto my ass.

"Lucy!"

Braden immediately bends down to me and protectively checks me over from head to toe.

"Braden! I am so sorry, I didn't even see you."

Cracking a warm smile, he lifts me up to my feet. His large arms wrap around me bringing me into his heavenly chest.

"It's ok, it happens. Where are you off to? You look nice."

Stepping back from me, Braden rakes his eyes up and down my body, stopping on my cleavage. From the way he felt them up last night, I can tell they are his favorite. I take a deep breath.

"I am going to dinner. My friend Kyle was supposed to meet me, but he is unfortunately not responding. I think he forgot or blew me off."

I avoid eye contact, embarrassed that I let him see me disappointed.

"I'll go with you."

Braden says immediately, not even hesitating. My eyes pop out of my brain and my stomach flips.

"Oh! You don't have to! I know you're probably busy."

I brush him off, but honestly, having him there would be nice. Going to a sit down restaurant alone, especially when I have a previous reservation for two, is a little embarrassing.

"I would love to go, Lucy. I just got off work and I'm hungry."

Braden stares at me with a heated gaze. It warms my stomach up so much I have to take a small step back from him just to think straight.

"Sure, I would really like that. Want to drive?"

I dig my purple keys out from my purse and hand them to him when he says yes. Wrapping his hand around mine, Braden pulls us toward the exit leading the way.

"Is it that new sushi place by the target?"

He asks while opening the passenger door for me and watching me get in.

"Yes! Fin's sushi. We have a reservation for two."

He nods, anger slightly in the back of his eyes. Braden shuts the door, enters on the other side, and turns the keys in the ignition. My leg heats up when he places his right hand on my upper thigh, squeezing it nonchalantly. That move goes straight to my core, making me feel all mushy inside.

When we get to the restaurant, Braden tells me to wait a second. He gets out of the car and jogs over to my side to open up the door. While stepping out of the car, I take a second to examine his sexy body. His grey henley top clings to his muscles in the most delicious way imaginable, while the dark jeans he is wearing make his thighs look large and strong. Licking my lips, I bring my eyes back up to his, and realize he is grinning at me because I am obviously checking him out.

"Wow, I didn't realize I looked that good."

Braden teases while threading his fingers through mine and pushing me up against the closed car door. My cheeks turn crimson, and I bury my head into his chest, taking in the woody smell of his body.

"Oops."

I reply. Braden and I linger in that intimate position for a few seconds before we pull away and walk hand and hand into the restaurant. We get inside and I notice all the Tokyo themed decor hung up on the walls and placed around the restaurant. Braden points to a model of Tokyo Skytree and we both awwe at the detail of it. We sit down and immediately, we both order Sake and look at the sushi menu.

"Usually I like to go to conveyor belt sushi because you can see all the options and then decide, but this place is so nice that I think anything will be great."

I say while browsing the tempura and wondering if I want any.

"I haven't had sushi since before I was incarcerated. I'm happy my first time after is with you. Want to get a few rolls and split them?"

Braden asks while smoothly tangling his feet with mine.

"Yes! I know I want the fried Philadelphia roll, but I am not sure about what else yet."

We end up ordering three rolls and some vegetable tempura to share. Hopefully, it won't be too much food.

"So, when is your next meeting with your parole officer? Do you have to prepare for it?"

Braden sighs and puts down his menu. I hope he doesn't feel uncomfortable talking about the meeting with me, I really just want to support him in any way possible.

"It is next week. I am not sure of the exact time yet, but I need to bring the form from my employer that says I am working. It will help me shorten my parole."

I nod and examine his features. Even though he looks daunting and brooding from the outside, I can tell he is actually nervous. I reach over to grab his hand for support, curling my hand around his gently.

"I am sure you will do great. Do you need to borrow my car for the meeting?"

Braden squeezes my hand and shakes his head no.

"It's ok Lucy, you are too kind. I can easily take public transportation."

I cross my arms, lean back in my seat, and shoot one eyebrow up. He looks surprised to see me in such a sassy way, but he needs to know that when I offer something, I mean it.

"Braden, take my car. It is way easier for you to go straight there. Plus, I saw your driving skills today and they seem good enough for you to take my car out alone."

He smiles and leans over the table to smooth out my propped up eyebrow and peck my cheek. His lips against my cheek send tingles down my body and I find myself starting to crave him. Before I can connect our lips, the sushi we ordered is delivered. Braden returns to his seat and we dive in.

I eat a couple bites of each roll, enjoying the flavor of the fish before moving onto the tempura. Best sushi ever. The homemade eel sauce that came with the rolls is so amazing, Braden and I fight over who can have the last dip. After convincing him, he lets me have the last bit of sauce. Dipping my final roll in, I devour the last of it.

I am so sucked into the delicious taste that I am surprised when Braden grabs my chin and gently wipes a dot of sauce off my lip with the pad of his thumb.

Licking my lips, I connect my eyes with him, immediately noticing his heated gaze. Little butterflies start to form in my stomach, as he slowly tucks a piece of my hair behind my ear. I can just imagine that pad of his thumb rubbing me until I can't focus.

We are so sucked into our little world that I don't notice the waiter standing to the side of us until he clears his throat multiple times to get our attention.

Annoyed, Braden removes his thumb from my lip and gets out his wallet to pay. I try to protest but he refuses, saying that he really wants to. As he is waiting for the server to print our receipt from the small table device, Braden's leg lightly skims across mine, sending tingles all the way up my legs to my core. I squirm a bit, trying to master the feeling that starts to tighten in my core. Again, his leg brushes mine, only this time, higher. I know that I need to get myself together, and I can't do that here, across from the hottest man I have ever laid eyes on. As soon as the waiter walks away, I grab my purse and walk swiftly to the bathroom, mentioning to Braden that I will be back in a minute.

Walking to the back of the restaurant, I take some deep breaths to try and calm myself down. Every time I am around Braden, I start to want to do things that are really inappropriate. I have never been in a relationship where I feel extremely desired or feel a large amount of sexual chemistry. Even in my last relationship, we had sex maybe once a week. It felt like we were more best friends than anything, so sex was just something we would do occasionally. With Braden, I feel confident and sexy, things I haven't totally felt with a man before. To have both a deep understanding of each other and tension is very overwhelming and exhilarating. All I want to do is rip his clothes off and have him make sweet, sweet love to me.

When I get to the gender neutral bathroom, I walk inside and close the door. Already, I am feeling more calm and ready to be back out there. Suddenly, I hear the turning of the door handle and I spin around to find Braden striding into the bathroom, slamming the door closed with his hand.

"Braden!"

I gasp, but before I can get anything else out, he presses his lips against mine and I melt against his kiss. He slowly moves his mouth down to my jaw, where he nips at my warm skin and then smooths it over with his soft tongue. Reaching down, he tightly grasps my thighs and places me on the counter beside the sink, pressing his body against mine. My nipples harden as they rub through the fabric of my dress onto his chest and I moan out from the amazing friction. He moves his lips down to my chest where he pulls the top of my sundress down, and swirls each of my nipples with his tongue. My hands find the bottom of his grey top, and I pull it off, throwing it to the ground. Braden chuckles quietly, and also reaches to the bottom of my sundress, pulling it up and off my body, only leaving me in my black lacy panties. Instinctively, I cross my arms over my body, not being used to being naked around him. With his large palms, Braden moves my hands away, whispering,

"It's just me baby, you're beautiful"

His leg moves to between your thighs and I slowly grind against it, trying to get more friction against me. I let out a breathy moan and buck against him when he presses the pad of his thumb against my clothed core. His finger teases my clit just before he pushes my underwear aside and plunges his long, thick finger inside me. He moves his finger in and out of my opening, slowly adding another finger, and then another. I cry out at the pleasurable stretching of my pussy, and I lean back against the mirror, moving my hips back and forth against him.

"So tight and wet"

He breathes, and I vaguely nod, too distracted with the tightness forming in my stomach. Braden speeds up, pulling his fingers out and in. My head falls back, and I writhe against him as my orgasm explodes. My legs shake and I moan so loud, he has to cover my mouth with the hand that is not inside me. Slowing down, Braden gently removes his fingers from me and dives down to capture my lips in a delicious kiss. After a few seconds of kissing him, my brain clears, and all that is on my mind is his erection that is straining against my thigh.

I reach down unbuckling his belt, when he stops my hands from moving.

"Lucy, you don't have to."

I shake my head at him and drop down off the counter onto my knees in front of him. I unzip his pants, and pull down both his boxers and pants in one go. His cock springs out from under the fabric and I marvel at the size of him. I reach out, taking him into my hand, and pump him a few times with the bead of precum at the top lubricating him. After a few seconds, I slowly take him into my mouth, swirling my tongue around the tip before sucking his whole length into my mouth. He groans and leans against the counter, gripping at the sides.

"Shit, Lucy."

I move my mouth up and down his length slowly at first, and then gradually faster, making sure to spend a few moments focusing on the tip. Braden moves his hips against my mouth, gently thrusting his cock deeper and deeper inside my wet, full mouth. When he hits the back of my throat, he moans out,

"I'm close, pull out Lucy."

I do no such thing. I suck his cock faster and harder until he is trembling and moaning underneath me. He takes a deep breath, and then a sticky, salty substance shoots into my mouth and fills me up. I swallow all of it quickly and lick my lips looking up at him.

As soon as we make eye contact, he reaches down to me, pulls me up and connects our lips in a searing kiss. A few heated seconds pass, and I pull back, wrapping my arms around him.

"You were amazing. I secretly dreamed about you on your knees in front of me, sucking my cock, naked, as soon as I met you for the first time."

I blush at Braden's words and pull away to pick up my dress from the floor. Both of us get dressed and smooth out our hair, making sure we look put together. Braden grabs my hand, and leads us out to the car, making sure that I am right next to him the whole time. When in the car, he places his hand on my leg comfortably and we chat about mundane things, like how his work is going, until we pull up to the building. Braden says he will walk me to my door, so we walk into the elevator together, his arm wrapped around my body so that I am as close as possible to him. On the ride up, he places little kisses on my cheeks and nose, claiming that I have the 'cutest face he has ever seen'. These kind words leave me feeling so happy. Nothing can break this feeling of warmth and love, until I see an angry Kyle leaning against my door, staring menacingly at Braden with his hand around my body.

Chapter 13

"Kyle.... What are you doing here?"

I ask, noticing the way that Braden's arm tightens around me as we approach him.

"What the FUCK Lucy! We make plans to go out and then you ditch me for a random guy!"

Kyle exclaims angrily, while stepping forward towards me. Braden responds quickly by pulling my body slightly behind his and pushing me against him. Rolling my eyes at his protectiveness, I step out from behind him and cross my arms at Kyle.

"Kyle. I was not the one who ditched, you were! I sent you multiple texts during the day and you did not respond."

He sighs and rubs his eyebrows aggressively.

"Lucy, MY PHONE DIED! When I got off work, my phone was dead. I drove here hoping to catch you before you left, but when I arrived, I saw you pulling out of the parking lot with another guy! HOW THE FUCK DO YOU THINK THAT MAKES ME FEEL HUH?

Kyle starts to yell and I step backwards into Braden's awaiting arms.

"Hey! Don't talk to her like that. You were the one that ghosted her. She did nothing wrong. It was a misunderstanding!"

Braden wraps a comforting arm around me, and steps forward toward Kyle to defend me.

"Shut the fuck up man. You knew we were going out and you sabotaged it! You're such an asshole."

Kyle shouts and clenches his fist. Both Braden and Kyle inch closer to each other, having a stare down. It's amusing to see both of them in a stance like this, especially when Braden is five inches taller than Kyle and has double the amount of toned muscles. The energy gets so intense that I have to step in between them.

"Look Kyle, I'm sorry that this happened. It was a misunderstanding, and it is no one's fault. There is no reason to get mad at Braden, he made me feel better and made my night great. As my friend, you should be happy about that."

Kyle rolls his eyes and crosses his arms, backing up a little.

"Kyle, I am going to bed. I understand your frustration with the situation, but there is no reason to yell and act like a child. I deal with enough temper tantrums at work and I don't need to deal with another one at home. Maybe we will reschedule, I'll have to think about it."

I turn to face Braden, who is still worked up about the situation, but has calmed down a little. Wrapping my arms around his neck, I lean in and press a warm kiss to his cheek. Braden grunts, and redirects our position so he can kiss me deeply and lovingly on the lips. After a few seconds of increasingly passionate kisses, I remember Kyle is there. I pull away from Braden and wish him a good night with another quick cheek kiss. I turn around heading for the door, noticing how Kyle is leaning against the wall with his arms crossed, shooting deadly daggers at Braden. I send a quick head nod to Kyle and enter my apartment, locking the door behind me.

POV Braden

As soon as my Lucy gets inside her apartment, I turn to face Kyle who has been aggressively staring at me ever since Lucy kissed me goodnight.

"Why the hell are you so angry?"

I ask nonchalantly. If I remember correctly, this is the guy that cheated on Lucy and broke her heart. He deserves every feeling of hurt he is getting right now.

"In case you don't know, Lucy and I have been together since high school. After a year apart, it is time we get back together. I don't understand why she is spending her time on you of all people."

Kyle says while uncrossing his arms and inching closer to me.

"In case you don't remember, asshole, you cheated on her. It's your fault that the relationship ended, and by the way you acted tonight, she's glad it did. You are aggressive and flaky. Grow up."

I say to him calmly while leaning relaxed against the wall. I've had confrontations with people 10X more intimidating than this preppy spoiled boy.

"Who are you to talk? You met her in jail."

I stiffen and squint my eyes at him, giving him the deadliest stare I can muster. How dare he talk to me like that.

"You better shut your damn mouth."

I threaten slowly. He chuckles darkly.

"You'll see. I'm going to win Lucy back. I won't stop trying until she says she will get back with me."

How disrespectful that he won't even account for how Lucy is feeling. Even with the strong feelings I have for her, I would walk away if she asked. I would never force her into anything. Of course I will fight like hell for her though.

"You better watch it, Lucy is mine."

I growl, pushing a finger into his chest for impact. Again, Kyle laughs lowly.

"We'll see."

Kyle gives me a death glare and leaves to walk down the hallway, ominous and brewing. I clench my fist and take some deep breaths. If he comes near my Lucy again, I don't know if I'll be able to hold back. Something about Lucy makes all my protective instincts go on high alert. I care for her so much, I don't want that manipulating bastard to hurt her again.

Lucy's POV

Walking into the kitchen at 4pm a few days later, I see Kiera and Michelle cooking away in the kitchen with food spread out all over the counters.

"Good Morning Sleepyhead!"

Both Kiera and Michelle greet while cutting up different vegetables. Last night, the emergency unit at my clinic was short staffed, so I ended up staying until six am. Exhausted, I slept in all day.

"What are you guys up to? It looks like a grocery store threw up all over this kitchen!"

I say while plopping down on one of the bar stools.

"We are making dinner because we invited Braden over for dinner."

Michelle says cooly, turning around to drop some cut potatoes into a pot on the stove. I freeze.

"WHAT! When? Why?"

I exclaim immediately hopping up from the bar stool and frantically combing out my hair with my fingers.

"Relax, he is coming in an hour. Michelle and I have been wanting to meet him ever since you started writing to him, but you never introduced us. We are taking matters into our own hands."

I roll my eyes and sit back down on the stool again.

"You could have just told me!? I would have invited him over!"

"Every time we bring him up, you blush and stumble over your words. And, if we talked to you about it first, you never would have said yes."

I sigh and begrudgingly agree.

"I guess. Do you need any help? What are you making?"

Michelle and Kiera brush me off.

"We are making shepherds pie, and no we don't need help. Go shower! We can smell you from all the way over here."

Kiera says lightheartedly while stirring the pot on the stove. I laugh and blame the smell on the broccoli that is cooking. Walking into my room, I start getting ready for this dinner by showering and picking out an outfit. Hopefully tonight goes well. Even though Kiera and Michelle are the most supportive friends I have, they are very judgmental of any boys that I bring around. I know they want the best for me, but it can get kind of annoying. I think they will like Braden though. He really is the most thoughtful guy I have been with, not to mention his amazing sex appeal. Just thinking about him turns me on.

Flashes of his strong body, his gorgeous chiseled face, and his thick cock appear in my mind. It doesn't help my horniness that I am currently in the shower where I can easily picture his hard body on mine. His hand gripping my hair and round ass as he grinds into me against the shower wall. I run my hands through the soft strands of his hair and brush my tongue along his sexy lower lip.

My hand makes its way down to my folds and my finger starts rubbing my clit in slow circles.

Wrapping my legs around his thick thighs, I rub my core against his long erection, moaning at the friction. He positions himself at my entrance, and the tip of his cock rubs sensually against my sensitive clit.

My finger moves quicker and faster, and I feel the knot in my stomach build inside me.

Braden looks deeply into my eyes and thrusts into me at a slow but intense pace. I cry out at the thickness of him filling me up. Braden gives me a moment to adjust and then slips out and thrusts quickly back in. Braden attaches his lips to my neck and sucks as he thrusts in and out of me at an addicting pace.

I start to feel a heartbeat in my clit until the knot inside my stomach explodes and I feel sticky wetness on my fingers. I take a deep breath and center myself, trying to to be embarrassed that I just came at the thought of him. After washing my hand off in the shower water, I complete my shower routine.

While drying off I decide to wear leggings and a white sweater, simple but still cozy. A few minutes later, I walk out of my room and jump into helping Kiera and Michelle cook. After helping assemble the pie, I hear the doorbell ring and I rush to answer it. Immediately, I am wrapped up in woodsy smelling arms and receiving kisses all over my face. I wrap my legs around Braden's waist and pull his face close to mine so I can plant my lips on his. Responding immediately, Braden bites my lip gently and uses his tongue to sooth over it. Michelle clears her throat audibly and I pull back, embarrassed. Braden reluctantly sets me down, but leaves one arm wrapped around me. I blush even more when he secretly grabs and squeezes my butt. I jokingly slap his chest and turn to face Michelle and Kiera.

"Sorry."

I apologize and rub my cheeks trying to hide the redness.

"Well, glad to see that you have the physical connection. Hey Braden, how are you doing?"

Michelle says while going in for a hug. Braden responds with a little hug for both Michelle and Kiera. I grab the wine from his hand and go dig out the opener from the drawer behind the island.

"I'm doing well, thanks! I was surprised when I was invited over, but I could not be happier to spend time with you guys."

I pop the bottle open and start pouring the wine into the glasses that Kiera just brought from the cupboard.

"Braden, you want some?"

I ask while extending him a glass. He nods, grabs the glass from my hand, and comes to stand next to me.

"Thanks baby. Do you guys need any help cooking?"

Michelle shakes her head and pulls out the pie, setting it on top of the stove.

"Nope! All done! Plates are right here, feel free to dish up."

Kiera leads the way, piling a heap of shepherd's pie on her plate and grabbing a few broccoli. Michelle, me, and Braden follow next, Braden insisting I go before him. After we all have dished up, we sit down at the table in the living room and enjoy the food. We all engage in small talk, Kiera asks how work is going for Braden and I ask Michelle if she has any exciting cases right now.

"Hey Lucy, your birthday is coming up next week, is there anything special you want to do?"

Michelle asks while holding Kiera's hand and taking a bite of mashed potatoes.

"What! Why didn't you tell me your birthday is next week!"

Braden exclaims excitedly while squeezing my thigh under the table. I shrug and think for a minute trying to decide what I want to do. Honestly, this coming week is going to be crazy busy for me. I have taken on way more hours this week because we are understaffed, so by the time my birthday rolls around next Friday, I will be exhausted.

"Probably just a party here, I won't want to go out after work."

I reply, taking a sip of wine. Michelle and Kiera lock gazes and look concerned.

"Ummmm Lucy, do you think that's really a good idea after last time?"

Kiera asks unabashed, staring at me. Braden turns to me puzzled, and asks,

"Luce, what happened last time?"

My breath catches in my throat and Michelle and Kiera's eyes bug out after realizing what they just revealed. I try to act cool about it, but my voice shakes.

"N-Nothing! I-It wasn't that big of a deal."

Kiera rolls her eyes and slams her hand down on the table.

"Getting drugged and almost sexually assaulted is not nothing Lucy!"

Kiera yells while Michelle crosses her arms and nods harshly at me. Braden's hand on my thigh freezes in place.

"WHAT."

Braden raises his voice and stares at me.

"What the hell are you talking about?!"

He exclaims, face getting red and muscles tensing.

"I was okay! I pushed him off and fell asleep, nothing happened!"

I try to reassure him, putting my hand on his chest. Under my palm, I can feel his heart pounding and his chest getting hot.

"Baby, why the fuck didn't you tell me!"

I gulp and look at an awkward Michelle and Kiera, silently asking them to give us a minute. They nod, grab our plates, and go to clean up.

"I'm sorry I didn't tell you Braden. I-I was embarrassed. I felt dirty and nervous that Michelle and Kiera would report it."

He squeezes my thigh with his left hand, and cups my cheek with the other.

"Why didn't you want them to report it. Sexual assault is no joke Lucy."

I sigh and look down.

"I didn't want to relive those memories, and I was worried that the person who did it would find out I was telling people. I was scared."

Braden immediately wraps me up into his arms and brings me into his protective chest. I take a few deep breaths of his pine scent and play with the hem of his hunter green sweater to calm my nerves.

"Lucy, I promise you that you will never be put in that situation again. I will be there for you. If you want to have another party here, I will be by your side the whole time looking out for you."

Smiling, I pull away from his arms and press a warm and loving kiss onto his awaiting lips. We refrain from deepening the kiss because Kiera and Michelle are in the same room, but there is no doubt that we want to make out for longer. After a few seconds, we pull away and rejoin Kiera and Michelle in the kitchen. They welcome us into their conversation and offer to fill our glasses with wine. Both of us nod, and we spend the rest of the night talking about more lighthearted business.

When I start yawning, Braden says that it is time to go. Michelle and Kiera give him a happy hug and tell him that he can come over for dinner any time. After they disappear into their room, I reach up to connect Braden and I's lips, something I have been waiting to do for the whole night. Finally, we are uninterrupted and it's time. Braden reaches around my hips and kneads my ass, making sure to spank each cheek a couple of times, probably leaving little red marks. I moan into his mouth, reach down, and rub him slowly through the outside of his jeans. As I drag a finger from the base of his clothed cock to the tip, I feel him harden under me. He groans, and presses my pelvis against him, creating intoxicating friction that makes my clit pound. Out of nowhere though, I yawn against his lips. Immediately, he stops and pulls away.

"You tired baby?"

He giggles and places a kiss on both of my cheeks.

"No!"

I say, trying to hide another yawn that I can feel coming. He chuckles again and places his forehead against mine.

"It's ok, we can finish this another night. Or i'll finish this alone... just with the thought of you."

He reaches down and palms his cock that is still straining against his jeans. I blush and ask,

"You think of me, when you .... take care of business?"

Braden slowly skims his lips down my neck and places open mouthed kisses from my ear to my collar bone.

"Yes. In the shower, in my bed, one time on the couch. I can't wait to actually have you in those places."

"Baby.."

I moan when he sucks on a sensitive spot right under my ear. Braden groans and takes a deep breath.

"I love it when you call me that. Just hearing you moan 'Baby' makes me want to come."

He gives me one last kiss on my lips and pulls away from me.

"I'll see you soon my Lucy, let me know when you decide to host your party. I can't wait to shower you with all kinds of gifts."

Braden smirks, gives my cheek another kiss, and walks out the door. I have a feeling the gifts he will give me will be ones we share in my bedroom.

Chapter 14

Warning, this chapter is a little smutty!

The day of my birthday, everything falls into place work-wise. A few nurses from the local hospital's emergency ward are transferring over for the week, which lets me get off early for my birthday. Earlier this week, I decided that it would actually be more work to host a party, so I decided I wanted to go out to a bar with the ladies and Braden. I think it was the right decision, I am tired after work today. When my shift is over, I hop into the car and head home.

As soon as I arrive at the apartment, I hop in the shower, scrubbing myself with my lavender vanilla body wash. I am applying some vanilla lotion in my towel when the doorbell rings. Michelle and Kiera are taking Rufus on a walk before we are gone for the night, so it is up to me to get the door. Quickly, I change into my satin robe, and pull open the apartment door. Standing behind it is gorgeous Braden. Dressed in a black henley top and dark jeans, he is looking absolutely seductive. Braden takes one look at my robe and smirks, stepping into the apartment.

"Happy birthday Lucy!"

I giggle and loop my arms around his broad shoulders, cuddling my wet hair into his chest.

"You're here early! I am not ready yet and Michelle and Kiera aren't home yet."

I say, pulling back from his arms to look up at him. Braden leans down to press a kiss on my cheek and murmurs in my ear,

"I know baby, I just wanted to see you before we go out on your special day. I also have a gift for you."

Braden caresses the tips of my wet hair with his fingers and I sigh.

"That sounds nice. I still have to get ready, but you could sit on my bed and we can talk while I primp?"

I invite. He smiles widely and kisses my forehead.

"I would love that. I've never seen your room before!"

Braden says as he holds my hand and follows me over to my bedroom.

"Well, welcome then! Sorry it's a little messy, I just got out of the shower when you knocked."

He looks around, taking in every detail.

"Lucy, your room is so nice. I love all your pictures on the walls. Is this you and Kiera in college?"

He asks, pointing to a framed photo of Kiera and I sitting on my nightstand. I nod. Braden looks at the other photo sitting on my nightstand as well.

"Are these your parents? I remember you saying you lost them."

"Yes, a few years ago in a car wreck. That photo is one of the last times we were together."

He runs his hands through my hair and pulls me into a comforting hug. We stay there for a few seconds, just taking in the feeling of each other. Something about Braden's hugs make me feel so protected and loved. I could stay in his embrace forever. Pulling back, Braden whispers to me,

"Lucy, if you ever need to talk or let your feelings out, know that I would love to be there for you."

I smile at him.

"Thank you. I really appreciate that."

Braden gives me one last kiss on the cheek and I pull away from him.

"Okay Mister! You are distracting me, I need to get ready."

Walking to my vanity, I plop down on the stool and pull out my moisturizer. I rub it all over my face and start my makeup. Behind me, I see Braden sitting on my bed and staring at me through the mirror. His sexy eyes are so tempting, I love the way he looks at me. I swallow. Braden's eyes scan down my body and settle on my breasts that peak out from the top of my soft silk robe. He lingers there for a few seconds, biting his lips, and sitting forward over his knees. That stance is so intense and sensual, I pause my makeup and turn to look at him. Breathless, I ask,

"What?"

"I want to give you your birthday present."

He states, walking out of the room into the kitchen. A few seconds later, Braden returns with a present that he must have brought with him.

"Aww baby, you didn't have to!"

I exclaim. I take the present from his hands and walk over to sit next to him on the bed. Slowly I unwrap the gift, tearing the green and blue wrapping paper. When I see what's inside, my heart stops and my core pounds. Resting beneath the paper is a black bullet vibrator. I turn to look at him and meet his intense stare.

"I wanted to get this for you because I want you to have maximum pleasure. Have you ever tried one?"

Braden asks while slowly pulling down the sleeve of my robe. Leaning down, he places delicious openmouthed kisses from behind my ear down to my collarbone. I resist a moan when he lightly grazes his teeth over my skin.

"Never, but I-I would like to try one. How do I use it?"

I ask embarrassed, slightly leaning into him.

"Don't worry, I'll use it on you the first time."

I can't wait a moment longer. I lean up and connect our lips in a searing kiss. Braden kisses me gently for a minute, letting me know that it's ok if I want to stop, and then brushes his tongue along mine. I bite down on his bottom lip, pulling on it slightly. This causes him to groan, and he pushes me backwards onto the bed. Braden hungrily unties my robe, and quickly pushes it down off my body. The calluses on his hands feel so good scraping and massaging my body. I reach up to try to take his shirt off, but he pins my hands to the bed.

"It's your birthday, and that means you only receive baby."

Braden dives down and connects his mouth to my right breast, sucking and licking my nipple in a way that makes my back arch.

"Mmmmmm"

I moan out loudly. Braden chuckles against my breast, and moves to give the other one the same treatment. I open my legs and grind my hips trying to get some sort of friction against my clit. Braden pulls back for a second and reaches over to grab the box. Popping the top off, he reaches inside and takes out the sex toy.

It's black, sleek, and looks about the size of a dick. Braden makes eye contact with me, and I nod. He presses the on button and the toy immediately buzzes to life. Leaning down over me, Braden brings his lips to mine again. I reach up and run my hands through his hair, trying to get as close to him as possible. Braden disconnects our lips and holds the buzzing toy in front of my mouth.

"Suck baby girl."

Braden orders. I take a second to study the vibrator before I slowly lean forward and wrap my lips over the tip. Connecting my eyes with his, I take the rest of the vibrator into my mouth. I run my tongue over the material several times to wet it, all while keeping my heated gaze with Braden.

Just by taking a quick look down, I can see how much this is affecting him, but he makes no move to stroke himself. After a few seconds, I let the toy go with a 'pop'. He smirks, and sensually moves the toy down to connect with my hard left nipple. Immediately when it touches me, I close my eyes, taking in the euphoric feeling.

"Fuck, Braden that feels great."

He huffs a laugh and connects the vibrator to my other nipple. The vibrations send shockwaves through my body, making me feel new things in my lower region. Licking his lips, Braden slowly slides the vibrator down between my breasts, over my stomach, and stops it just before it reaches my clit. Sucking in a breath, I wiggle a little trying to get it to move down a few inches.

He chuckles warmly and moves the vibrator right where I want it. As soon as it presses against my clit, my lower region squirms. The vibrations are so much more intense than anything I've ever felt before. My hands reach up and dig into the back of Braden's sweater, raking up and down his back trying to grasp some semblance of control. Braden leans down and connects our mouths as he circles the vibrator around my clit. These small circles catch my breath and I throw my head back and a gasp escapes my mouth.

"Does that feel good baby?" Braden gravelly whispers into my ear. I absent-mindedly nod, focusing on the ever tightening knot in my lower abdomen. He starts to move the bullet vibrator in and out of my entrance, and I close my eyes. Suddenly, he turns off the vibrator. I open my eyes, and look at him confused.

"Get on all fours Lucy."

I thickly swallow and nod. Turning around, I get to my hands and knees, my pussy facing him.

"That's better"

Braden mumbles. Without warning he turns the toy on again and attaches it to my clit. I cry out and clutch the sheets. Braden rubs the vibrator in figure eights around my clit, alternating between fast and slow. The only sounds coming out of my mouth are garbled moans and cries. Moving from my clit to my pussy, he pushes the thick toy inside my entrance. Slowly he pushes in and out, then increases his pace.

"Uh yes.."

I moan out, bending forward so my breasts are pressed against my bed and my ass is straight up in the air. With encouragement, Braden moves the toy in and out of me at a rapid rate. Clenching around the toy, the knot in my stomach explodes, and my body goes crazy. My thighs shake and I scream out,

"Braden!"

But he doesn't stop. He keeps pounding the toy in and out of my pussy at a gut wrenchingly delicious speed.

"Just let go Lucy, I got you."

I take a deep breath and do as he says. As soon as I relax my body, a wet substance exits out of my pussy and runs down my thighs. I hardly notice though, as I collapse on the bed and recover from the intense orgasm I just had. Braden turns off the vibrator and places it next to us on the bed. Afterwards, he goes into the bathroom and brings back a wet washcloth. Braden turns me on my back and wipes up my thighs gently, pressing little kisses to the insides of them. Throwing the dirty washcloth into my hamper, he reaches up to cup my face and presses a few warm kisses to my neck and face.

"Baby, you squirted."

Braden mumbles into my ear as he lovingly runs his hands through my hair. I turn to lay my head on his chest, and look him in the eyes.

"What? What's that?"

Braden connects his lips to my cheek again and says into my ear,

"You came so hard, you squirted."

Suddenly my mind becomes clear and I lift my head up.

"Woah. I don't think I've ever done that."

He immediately breaks out into a smile and wraps me up in his arms, bringing me closer to his body.

"Is it bad that I have a sense of satisfaction that I made you feel that way?"

I shake my head no and lean my head back onto his chest. We stay there for a while, just enjoying the feeling of cuddling together. Suddenly, a knock on the bedroom door breaks us out of our trance.

"Lovebirds, we leave in half an hour. You better be ready, birthday girl!"

I sigh into Bradens warm chest, give him one last cuddle, and then get up from the bed. My legs are a little tired and not fully recovered from my blinding orgasm, so I stumble a little when I walk over to the closet. When I hear Braden chuckle behind me at my jelly legs, I turn and playfully glare at him.

"Oh, be quiet!"

I roll my eyes. He just smirks and tucks one arm behind his head, slowly running his eyes down my fully naked body. Turning from his heated gaze, I grab a little black dress from my closet and pull it on. I love this dress. It has ruching around my breasts to make them pronounced, but the rest of the dress is loose silk. Super flattering. After my dress is on, I sit down at my vanity, again, and actually do my makeup. Because I don't have that much time to get ready, I keep the makeup simple. When done, I reach for my hairbrush and start to comb through my mostly air-dried hair. Out of the corner of my eye, I see Braden get up from the bed and come over to me. Gently, Braden takes the brush out of my hands and starts to tenderly run the comb through my hair.

"Let me do it baby."

He whispers in my ear and places a quick kiss on my neck. Continuing to brush through my hair, Braden takes extra care to not pull at my head. When he encounters a snarl, he works through it softly, running the comb over it a couple times. When Braden is done, he places the brush on the counter and wraps his arms around me from behind.

"Almost ready?"

"Yes! I just have to put my shoes on."

I respond, standing out of his arms and picking up my black heels from the floor. A few minutes later, Michelle, Kiera, Braden, and I leave for the bar. Michelle offers to DD, so we take her car.

When we arrive, I notice how nice the bar is. Inside there is a theme of crystal chandeliers, red carpet, and different colored lights surrounding the bar and the dance floor. Immediately, we all go to the bar to get our first round. I try to help pay for the first round of tequila shots, but as soon as I slide my card over to the Bartender, Kiera and Braden object.

"Woah!"

They say in unison.

"Lucy, no way in hell you're paying tonight! It's your birthday!"

Braden says, trying to announce over the loud music. Kiera nods her head to agree. I lean into Braden's ear and place my hand on his chest.

"You already got me a gift, remember?"

I am not that good at flirting to get what I want, so I can feel my cheeks turn bright red. Braden huffs, and slowly reaches down to wrap his large hands around my waist.

"My Lucy, if you think that you are only getting one gift from me for your birthday, you are mistaken."

He reaches into his pocket and hands the bartender his card for the tab. Knowing that I lost, I roll my eyes and tell Braden thank you.

A few shots later, I feel myself letting loose. Kiera has started telling funny stories about me in college, and I can't stop laughing. Braden's favorite story is the one where I took a hit for the first time and made mac and cheese in the middle of a house party. The night is going so well. I feel so lucky to have these wonderful people in my life.

"Lucy, I gotta pee. Wanna come?"

Kiera says, obviously looking uncomfortable. She keeps squirming in her seat. I laugh and agree.

"I'll come too, the doors to these bathrooms don't lock all the way. I can hold both your doors closed."

Michelle says, getting up and smoothing out her dress.

"I'll watch the table and get us another round!"

Braden says, taking another sip of his beer. Reaching down, I connect my lips with his quickly.

"Will you watch my purse?"

I ask, pulling away from him. He nods and grabs my purse from my outstretched hands. Kiera, Michelle, and I have to wait a few minutes in line, but thankfully not too long. By how fast Kiera ran into the stall when it was her turn, I would say it was a close one. Michelle and I laugh, and then I use the next available stall. I wash my hands and smooth down my dress in the mirror, noticing a loose thread and pulling it off.

"Ready?"

Michelle asks us. Kiera and I nod, and we all head out of the bathroom towards the table. As soon as I see Braden though, my heart stops. A leggy brunette is sitting next to him, whispering in his ear and grabbing his bicep. Suddenly, Braden and I make eye contact, and his eyes widen.

Chapter 15

I don't believe what I'm seeing. How could Braden think it was okay to be that close to another girl. I guess we haven't put a label on us or anything, but from the way we act together, I thought we were exclusive. My eyes water and I angrily wipe away any tears that start to well up in my eyes. On my birthday too!

Quickly, I snatch my purse that is sitting next to the brunette at the table and run outside, avoiding all eye contact with him.

"Lucy, wait!"

Braden yells from behind me. I can tell that he is following me, but I could care less. All I want to do is go home and curl up with Rufus. I am just about to try to open Michelle's car when Braden places his hand on my wrist and spins me around.

"Lucy, baby, it's not what you think."

I roll my eyes at him and try to push him away. He doesn't budge and looks around outside in a worried manner.

"Braden, in case you don't remember, I've heard those words before. I'm not stupid."

He lets out a deep breath and cups my cheek with his hands.

"Lucy, listen to me. Something is happening and I need you to go home right now. I'll meet you at the apartment where I will explain everything."

Once again, Braden looks around our surroundings for something. I follow his gaze, but don't see anything out of the ordinary.

"What the fuck are you talking about?"

Braden presses a kiss on my forehead and takes a step back from me.

"Please, go. It's not safe here. I'll meet you at your apartment. Stick with Michelle and Kiera, don't get separated."

With that, Braden runs back inside, leaving me, Michelle, and Kiera outside. I make eye contact with them and we all get into the now unlocked car.

"What's going on?"

Michelle asks, gripping Kiera's thigh across the center council nervously.

"I'm not sure. Braden said 'It's not safe here' and encouraged us to go home. This can't be a cover up for flirting with another girl, right? I mean it's a kind of obscure way to get out of something."

Kiera shakes her head and crosses her arms. The only lights in the back of the car are the headlights of passing cars.

"It's pretty elaborate. When you ran out, I kind of caught the end of their conversation. The brunette said something like 'so that's the girl we've seen you with', but I didn't hear anything else."

I furrow my eyebrows in confusion.

"Who's we? People have been watching us?"

Michelle parks in front of our building and we all briskly walk into the front of the entrance. Once we enter the apartment, I sigh, making sure to double check that the door is locked. Kiera brings me into a warm, comforting hug while Michelle firmly rubs my back.

"It will all be okay Lucy. I am sure he has an explanation. From what I've seen, he isn't the kind of guy to flirt with another girl in the same bar as you."

I take a deep breath, trying to calm myself. A few minutes of comforting later, I hear a firm knock at the front door.

"Lucy, it's me."

Braden calls from the outside of the door. Stepping away from Kiera and Michelle, I walk over to the door and open it. Immediately, Braden wraps his arms around me. This embrace is different from earlier tonight, it is more protective and desperate.

"Lucy,"

Braden breathes. I accept the hug for a few moments, but step out of his embrace. As soon as I leave his side, a look of sadness appears across his face.

"Explain."

I say, crossing my arms and raising an eyebrow at him. Braden sighs and leans against the wall, resting his hand on my hip just to keep physical contact with me.

"I-I know that girl. She was one of the people I took the fall for when I got sentenced."

My heart stutters a little. A look of surprise appears on both Michelle and Kiera's faces.

"I was part of a gang, the Seattle Cynicals. You know I grew up with no family, when they offered me a place in their group, I took it. I was young and didn't know what the reality of being in a gang was like. I became connected with them, but it was toxic. The group only loved me on their terms. When I started college, I met new people. Good people.

I realized that I didn't want to be in their group anymore. They refused to let me go, saying I knew too much. I left anyway and went into hiding after I graduated college. A while after I left, they got caught smuggling cocaine, and they all named me as their leader. I was convicted, while they got off with small punishments."

As Braden tells me his story, he avoids eye contact in shame. I can tell he is embarrassed, but I don't want him to be ashamed of his past around me.

"That girl is still part of The Cynicals. Her name is Sugar and she usually acts as the messenger. Apparently, the gang wants me back and will do anything to ensure that I join again.

I gulp and make contact with his worried gaze.

"Lucy, they saw us on both our dates. They know I care about you. I'm worried they are going to come after you."

I shake my head and lean into his inviting arms.

"But, there's no way in hell that I am letting them take you away from me. I will always be there to protect you."

"Us too Lucy!"

Michelle and Keira say. I nod my head at them thankfully and then non-verbally signal to them that I need some alone time with Braden. Both of them get the message and disappear into their room. I turn back to Braden and wrap my arms around his neck, just taking in the delicious scent of him.

"I was worried when I saw her all over you. I mean, we haven't..... made anything official yet, so technically you can do anything you want but, it hurt."

He reaches up and grabs my throat with his hand. His cold silver rings press into my warm neck, causing a shiver to run down my spine.

"Look at me Lucy."

I slowly make eye contact with his heated gaze.

"You are mine. Spending time with you is the best part of my days. I have not looked at another girl since I met you, they don't appeal to me. I only want you."

With his last line, he squeezes my throat gently but firmly, reminding my body that I am his.

"G-Good to know."

I breathe out. Swallowing, I push my hands through his dark locks, and slightly pull on the ends. I feel a hardness press up against my lower stomach. I roll my eyes and take my hands away from his hair.

"You have the sex drive of a teenager"

I giggle out. Braden groans and squishes me back into his chest.

"How am I supposed to not get aroused with you gripping onto my hair like that?"

He grumbles into my shoulder. Sighing, he makes eye contact with me and I notice his eyes have darkened.

"I don't think it's a good idea for you to be alone tonight. I think you will be safer if you stay with me tonight."

I smile excitedly and brush my hands down his muscular arms.

"At your place? I've never seen your place!"

Braden swallows nervously and takes another deep breath. It's almost like he is working up courage.

"Yes, want to stay at mine tonight?"

Immediately, I agree and go to grab my toothbrush from my room. We walk out the door together and take the elevator down one floor. Just before we enter his apartment, Braden stops and looks right into my eyes.

"Lucy, just a warning, I don't have a lot of ....furniture. I'm trying to save money, so it's not a lot."

Ah. So this is why he was nervous about bringing me back here. Reaching up, I cup Braden's face in my hands and place a kiss on his cheek. I feel him release a relieved breath.

"Braden, I'm sure what you have will be just perfect. I promise, I don't judge based on how much you have or don't have."

He nods, looks me in the eyes again, and then turns to unlock the door. The apartment is smaller than mine because it is a one bedroom. The living room has a blue couch, an oak coffee table, and a TV mounted on the wall. The kitchen is cute and quaint with a few plates by the sink and some mail sitting on the counter. To the left is the door to what I'm guessing is his bedroom.

"I love it. Braden, it's great."

Immediately, I see his face break out into a smile and he wraps me up into a hug.

"Thanks baby."

"Is that you're room?"

I tilt my head toward the door. Braden nods and then leads me over to the closed door. Inside the room, his neat grey bed sits in the middle, with a simple bedside table and lamp next to it. The bathroom door is open, and inside, there is a nice shower with a glass door.

"Are you tired yet?"

Braden asks while gently rubbing my back. I lean into his touch and sigh. I love when he plays with my hair and rubs my back. It reminds me of how my mom used to care for me.

"Yeah, I'm getting there."

He swallows almost disappointedly, nods, and pulls his henley over his head quickly. While he bends over to unbutton his jeans, I sit down on the bed and admire his delicious physique. I blatantly rake my eyes down his toned chest, loving how his abs tighten when he knows I'm checking him out. When he is only in his boxers, I gaze heatedly at his package, which is hidden just underneath. Biting my lip, I try to suppress a moan when he leans down to press a gentle kiss to my lips.

"I'm going to shower baby, get comfy. If you need water or a snack, it's in the kitchen."

He turns away from me and walks into the bathroom, only closing the door halfway. Sighing, I collapse backwards onto his bed. Mhmm, his covers are drenched in the amazing smell of him. Being surrounded by his scent turns me even more on.

I can feel my nipples start to grow hard under the fabric of my dress as I imagine him leaning over me and running his tongue down my breasts. Slowly, I shimmy out of my dress, unclasp my uncomfortable bra, and throw them into the corner of the room. Closing my eyes, I reach my hand down to brush against my wet, clothed, core. Gently at first, I rub circles over my clit, pretending it's Braden's fingers that are doing the massaging. Pushing my underwear off, I attach my fingers right to my clit. The direct contact brings a moan from my mouth.

Feverishly, I enter one finger into my dripping hole, and pump it in and out, trying to reach my g-spot. It's not enough. I need more. That half open door to the bathroom is starting to look like an invitation.

Am I ready to go all the way with Braden? We already did things before we went out, will he think I'm crazy if I want more? But I do. I really do want more. I need his thick length to fill me up and pump in and out of me until I'm squirming. Building my courage, I slowly pull my fingers out my wet, needy opening and walk to the bathroom entrance. I push the door open quietly and see him standing under the water, pumping his length at a fast rate, biting his knuckle to keep the sound of his moans in. I smile to myself. I guess Braden needs more too.

Without second guessing myself, I open the shower door and step under the warm water, making heated eye contact with Braden.

"Baby, what...."

He says huskily, slightly embarrassed but more turned on than anything.

"I-I want one more thing for my birthday."

I say, running my fingers down his strong arms to rest on his naked hips. He knowingly smirks and brings me closer to him under the running water.

"And what would that be?"

Braden whispers seductively into my ear. Swallowing, I mutter

"Fuck me."

Right after the words leave my lips, Braden lifts me up and wraps my thighs around his bare waist. Pinning me up against the cold shower wall, he presses his hard cock to my clit and connects our lips with a groan. Braden's hands reach down to knead my ass, squeezing it and rolling his hips against my clit, sending waves of pleasure down my body. He removes his lips from mine and kisses down my body stopping right between my heavy and aching breasts.

"I love these."

Braden whispers, his breath hitting my wet nipples, causing them to harden even more. A deep moan escapes me when his wet mouth attaches to my nipple, slightly scraping at it with his teeth. He then moves to the other nipple, working my bud with his tongue and his teeth. Placing me down on the tiled shower seat, Braden uses both hands to play with my breasts, kneading them and rolling the nipples until I am signing out.

At this level, his member is right in front of me. Leaning forward, I pump his length a few times before enveloping the head of his slightly leaking cock into my mouth. As soon as I run my tongue over his tip, he lets out a hiss and bucks his hips. Grabbing his strong thighs, I keep him in place as I take him deeper into my mouth. I massage his length with my tongue and take him all the way in until he hits the back of my throat.

"Shit, baby."

I giggle slightly around his length which makes him moan at the vibrations of my throat. Suddenly, Braden lifts me back up and presses me against the wall again, squishing my ass against the glass of the shower. Teasing, he runs the tip of his cock up and down my throbbing entrance.

"Oh my god."

I moan, gripping onto Braden's shoulders for support.

"Baby, my condoms are in my room."

I shake my head and grind up against his member.

"I have the implant and can you pull out?"

I ask, biting my lip. Braden nods and connects our eyes as he slowly pushes in, my pussy walls tightening around his cock.

"Mhmmmmm"

Braden growls loudly and grips my ass tightly. After a few moments, he pulls out and then thrusts in again slowly, and then faster. My hips start to move with his, meeting each of his deep thrusts. I kiss him passionately and scrape my nails down his back as he roughly pounds into me. Bringing his hand up to my neck, Braden chokes me gently but dominantly. I moan out.

"You like that baby? You like my hand wrapped around your neck as I fuck you?"

He slightly changes angles, grazing my cervix and pumping a wave of intense pleasure into me. I cry out, throwing my head back and closing my eyes. The pleasure builds and builds until I am a complete mess. My eyes are tightly shut as my legs shake and my nails dig into Braden's back.

"I'm coming."

I yell out. My orgasm explodes, erupting through my body and making my legs turn into jello. I squeeze my walls against him, encouraging him to find his release too. He grunts out, his thrusts becoming sloppy and sloppier.

"Where do you want me to come baby."

Braden groans out as he pulls out of me and pumps his length vigorously. I collapse to my knees and look up at him.

"O-On my tits."

I say, grabbing my breasts and pushing them upwards. A few seconds later, Braden lets out a loud, husky moan and releases all over my awaiting breasts. He pants, presses his hands against the shower wall and looks down at me. I make eye contact with him and slowly try to stand up. When he notices my tired legs, he smiles and pulls me up to his chest.

Connecting our lips, Braden kisses me lovingly, running his hands gently through my hair. He pulls away and reaches for the body wash that is on the metal hanging rack. Squirting some into his hand, he lathers me up and rinses his cum off me under the warm shower water. All I can do is admire his handsome face, and take in the amazing way he makes me feel. After both of us have rinsed off, we step out of the shower and towel off together.

Braden does not let me leave his side. As we brush our teeth and I put on his T-shirt, he keeps me at arms length, always pressing kisses to my face or shoulder. I can tell that even a few seconds after we became intimate in that shower, he has double the amount of possessiveness.

Together, we climb into bed and turn off the lights. Wrapping his hand around my waist, Braden brings me close to his body and presses my head into his chest.

"How are you feeling my love?"

He asks, running his hands over my arms in a comforting gesture. I sigh and smile into his chest.

"I'm not sure if I will be able to walk tomorrow, but other than that, I'm just perfect. You?"

Braden chuckles into my damps hair and kisses my cheek.

"Lucy."

I turn to face him and I meet his serious but caring gaze.

"I'm in love with you."

My heart stops. He loves me? It's so soon. I've only known him for three months.

"I just wanted to tell you, in case something happens and we are separated."

My stomach turns in a nervous way and my eyes pop open.

"You're leaving?"

I ask frantically. My grip on him becomes tighter and my breathing is faster.

"No! No Lucy. I don't want to leave you ever. But if something happens to me, I want you to know."

I bring him into a tight embrace and shake my head from side to side.

"Don't do anything stupid Braden. Try to avoid the gang, I want, no I need you here with me. I-I love you too."

Braden breaks out into a smile and connects our lips in a passionate kiss. Wrapping my arms around him, I bring him even closer, wanting to be pressed fully against him. Pulling back, I rest my head on his chest again and fall asleep to the feeling of him gently rubbing my back.

Hope you all had a good week!

Chapter 16

It's the first of October. I observe the gorgeous leaves fall off the trees lining the road while I listen to the ringing of my phone. My brother never picks up, so I'm not expecting anything. Because I've been so busy with Braden, I haven't felt as lonely. Dave, my brother, not being in contact with me hasn't been weighing on me as hard as usual. After a few rings, my call goes to voicemail like usual. This time though, I decide not to leave a message. If he doesn't want to pick up my calls, I won't bother him with a voice message.

"Babe, eggs are ready!"

Braden calls from the other room, bringing me out of my ruminating negative thoughts. As I walk into the kitchen, a smile grows onto my face when I remember what we did last night. I swear I can still feel his hands caressing my body and his hot mouth kissing my neck, breasts, and core.

"What are you smiling at?"

Braden asks cheekily while I grab the plate he offers me and dish up the amount of eggs I want.

"Nothing, just thinking about last night."

I sit up on his kitchen counter and start to stab some eggs with my fork. Yum, Braden is a great egg cooker.

"Oh yeah, what exactly about last night?"

Braden asks. He comes over to where I am sitting on the counter and places his deliciously strong arms on either side of my body. I make a smart decision and set my plate down to avoid any egg spillage. He leans into me and whispers,

"Were you thinking about the club, the drinks, or me fucking you against the shower wall?"

I swallow and make heated eye contact with him.

"Maybe the last one."

He smirks and presses a kiss to first my cheek, then my neck, and then the top of my breasts. Braden places a hand on my shoulder, pushes me back to lay on the counter, and separates my thighs with his firm grip.

"Mmmm baby maybe we should repeat that then?"

He slowly slides my panties off my legs and presses hot kisses on the inside of my thighs. As soon as his lips connect with my core, I hear a ringing from next to us on the counter.

"Ignore it."

Braden breathes onto my clit and drags his tongue over my bud. I nod my head and try to drown out the ringing sound by focusing on the amazing feeling of his tongue. The buzzing finally stops, but it starts up again as the person calling re-calls. Braden groans, detaches himself from my pussy, and reaches for my phone. As soon as he reads who is calling though, his face drops into an angry look.

"What?"

I sit up from my previous position and take the phone from him.

"Oh, it's Kyle. Why would he call twice?"

I'm confused. I'm still angry at Kyle but he isn't on his phone a lot. If he calls more than once, it's not just a call to say 'hey'. I look back up at Braden and he is still angrily staring at the phone.

"I feel like I should take it. He wouldn't call twice if it wasn't important, right?"

Braden rolls his eyes and gestures for me to take the call. I kiss his cheek and pick up the call.

"Hello?"

"Lucy? Hey."

"What's going on?"

I hear Kyle sigh and pause for a minute.

"Sorry for calling, I know you're still mad at me. I just need someone to talk to you. Something happened to my mom."

I make eye contact with Braden and give him a surprised look.

"What happened?"

"Her cancer relapsed. She just had a doctor's appointment where they found a growing tumor in her other breast."

"Shit, Kyle I'm sorry."

I hear him sniffle behind the phone and I start to feel bad. Yes, I hate how he reacted to seeing Braden and I, but this is different. It's Sherrie. She was always so nice to me. Especially after my parents died, she was there for me.

"Do you mind coming over?"

Kyle asks. I look over at Braden and purse my lips together.

"I'm kind of with Braden right now, Kyle. I can't -"

"Please Lucy! I need you right now."

Kyle says frantically into the phone. Again, I look over at Braden. He is clenching his fist in frustration.

"Fine, I'll be over soon."

"Yes! I mean yes thank you for coming to support me."

"See you soon."

"Bye Lucy."

I hang up the phone, place it on the counter, and rub my temples. That seemed weird. As soon as I mentioned that I'm with Braden, he was adamant on me leaving him and coming over. But at the same time, what if he is actually upset and needs help?

"I think I'm going to go see him."

I say out loud to Braden. He walks back over to me and pulls me in his arms.

"I know. Is it bad for me to not want you to go?"

I smile into his warm chest and shake my head.

"No, I get it. I feel bad but I don't really want to go. At the same time though, I really like Sherrie and she would want me to be there for her son."

Braden takes a deep breath and rubs my back comfortingly.

"Can I drive you there?"

My heart warms.

"I would love that. It might take a while to calm him down, are you sure you don't mind waiting?"

Braden leans down to connect our lips in a searing and passionate kiss. I reach up and play with his necklace as I enjoy the amazing feeling of his soft lips and tongue. He pulls back and leans his forehead on mine.

"No, I don't mind at all. Maybe I'll go get a coffee while you talk to him. Honestly, I feel better about being there just in case he tries something."

I give him a confused look and wrap my hands around his waist.

"Do you really think he would? I mean, he's seen us happily together. Not to mention you are double his size."

Braden kisses my cheek and tightens his grip on my hips.

"On the night he blew up at us in the hallway, we talked for a few minutes when you went inside. He said that he was going to try to get you back."

I pull away surprised and swallow.

"Really? He said that? We have been broken up for a year and I have completely moved on. The only reason I still talk to him is because I have been friends with his family for a long time. Does he not see how freaking in love I am with you?"

Braden smiles at the last part and kisses me feverishly all over my face.

"I love when you say that. But seriously baby, if he tries anything, call me and I will immediately pick you up."

I nod and walk back into the bedroom to get dressed. I grab all the things that I brought last night, but make sure to leave my toothbrush. Braden and I leave his apartment, walk to the parking garage and get into my car. I don't mind Braden driving my car. I am an anxious driver, so being in the passenger seat is more enjoyable for me anyways. Driving down the road, I admire Bradens arm that is placed on my thigh. I love his tattoos and veins, they make me feel so protected. I don't notice that we arrive until Braden takes the keys out of the ignition and turns to me.

"Remember, if he tries anything, call me immediately."

I nod, kiss him lovingly on the lips, and get out of the car. Knocking on the front door, I wait for Kyle to answer. A few seconds later the door is pulled open and I am enveloped in a hug.

"Lucy!"

I'm shocked and unmoving for a minute, but then wrap my arms around him to return the hug.

"Uhhh hey."

Kyle pulls back from me and gives me a warm smile. I return his smile with one of my own, then step back from his embrace. Before I forget, I turn around and wave at Braden who is staring intently out the driver's side window. He sends me a small smile and then slowly drives off. Turning around to face Kyle, I notice his furrowed eyebrows and clenched fist.

"What?"

I ask. Kyle just shakes his head and leads me into the house. It is pretty messy, clothes are strung up around the floor, there's beer cans in the corners, and some of the lightbulbs are out. It makes sense though, Kyle lives with three boys that he met in his frat in college. Kyle leads me up to his room and plops down on his bed. I sit down in his black desk chair and put my purse next to me on his Ikea desk.

"So, how are you feeling Kyle?"

I ask, trying to be a good friend. He shrugs and takes a long, deep, breath.

"It sucks. I thought we were done with her treatment, but she came back from the doctor today saying that she needs to have a scan. I'm nervous that they are going to find another tumor."

I lean forward on my knees and rest my head on my propped hand.

"I'm sorry, the anxiety of waiting to find out can be - wait didn't you say she was diagnosed over the phone?"

Kyle freezes momentarily, almost like he is caught off guard, and then relaxes back onto the bed.

"Oh well yes but we don't know for sure yet. Tomorrow is the confirmation scan."

I push aside my gut feeling that he is lying to me and send him a small smile.

"But anyways, can we talk about something else? I want to know how you are doing."

"Oh, I thought you wanted to talk about your mom, that's why I came over."

I say in a confused manner. Over the phone he seemed pretty distraught and in need of someone to vent to.

"Yeah, it's hard to talk about. It's nice to talk about something different to take my mind off things."

Kyle says stumbling over his words a little bit. He rises from his position from the bed and walks over to lean on the desk next to me.

"So, how have you been Lucy? Tell me about work and stuff just like old times."

I sigh and lean back in the chair. I thought I was going to be helping him deal with grief, not talking to him like we're still close. I know that some patients prefer to be distracted while going through hard circumstances, but we still aren't on the best terms. I think another person he knows would be better at distracting him.

"Um, I've been good. Pretty busy with work and Kiera, Michelle, and Braden."

He tenses slightly and leans back a little more on the desk. Making contact with my purse, Kyle knocks it off the desk, and my things go flying.

"Oh shit, sorry Lucy."

Kyle says while quickly bending down to pick up my items that spilled.

"Oh, it's ok! Here let me help."

I say starting to bend down to help pick things up.

"NO! I mean no, I got it. I made the mess, I should clean it up."

Kyle yells out. I flinch back a little.

"Umm, ok. You got it I guess."

Kyle takes a minute to put my stuff in the bag, stands up, and hands me my purse.

"Thanks."

I say nervously. It feels like I'm walking on eggshells around him. Ever since he yelled at me and Braden that night when we were supposed to get sushi, it seems that he has been pretty on edge. I pull out my phone discreetly and text Braden that I'm almost ready to go.

"Kyle, I wanted to ask you something."

Kyle looks at me surprised and then smirks, again leaning against the desk next to where I'm seated.

"Ask me anything Lucy."

I fiddle with my fingers nervously.

"I just wanted to make sure we're on the same page and that we are just friends. You aren't harboring any feelings from our past relationship, right?"

Kyle's smirk drops from his face and his lips turn into a tight line.

"Why do you ask?"

I switch from playing with my hands nervously to brushing through my hair with my fingers.

"I was just talking to Braden, and he said that after I went inside that one night, you told him that you still.. liked me. Is that true?"

Kyle frowns, clenches his fist, and leans over towards me.

"Well what if it was true? I know you still love me Lucy. We dated for so long, and you just move on with some tatted up douchebag! You are obviously rebounding because you are still in love with me."

I gasp and get up from my chair offended.

"Don't talk about Braden like that, he treats me really well. And let me assure you, I am totally moved on from you. Please, d-don't pursue me romantically anymore."

Kyle moves closer to me and wraps his arms around my waist. Scared, I try to pry his arms off my waist but he is too strong.

"I know you love me. Look, your heart rate is racing because I am this close to you."

Kyle takes one of his hands from my waist and pushes down on the pulse point in my neck. I try to back up from his revolting touch but he squeezes my waist painfully tight.

"Let me go. I don't want this."

Kyle's face turns red, and he angrily takes a hold of my wrists and aggressively pins me to the wall. He squeezes my wrists so tightly that a shooting pain erupts in my left wrist.

"Ouch, please stop Kyle."

Kyle smirks and leans in to press an unwanted kiss to my neck.

"I missed this position Lucy. Pretty soon you'll realize that I am the one for you, and that Braden ass will be in the past."

Mustering up all the strength that I have in my body, I use my leg to kick him right in the balls. Kyle cries out and loosens his grip on my wrists. Quickly, I pry myself out of his grasp, grab my purse, run down the stairs and out the door, hoping that Braden is outside the house. Thankfully, he is. I run to the car, fling open the door with my not hurting hand, and get into the car.

"Go, go now."

I say nervously to Braden as I buckle my seat belt. He starts the car and immediately drives off.

"Baby, what happened. Did he touch you? I swear I'm going to kill that motherfucker."

Instinctively, I reach over to hold Braden's hand but then remember that my wrist hurts. I cry out quietly, cradling my wrist.

"Are you hurt?! What happened? Did he do that?"

Braden is now frantically asking me questions, obviously trying to hold back the urge to turn the car around and beat him up.

"He just got really handsy, and he squeezed my wrist too hard."

Braden revs the engine and speeds home, weaving through cars and racing through yellow lights.

"HANDSY! Baby, I swear. Once I get your wrist taken care of, I'm going to beat this little shit up."

He parks in the parking garage and gets out of the car, slamming the door. Before I know it, he opens my door and picks me up in his arms.

"I can walk Braden, it's only my wrist that hurts."

He just shakes his head and carries me through the complex all the way to his place. I cuddle into his chest, enjoying the feeling of being safe and cared for. When we enter his apartment, he places me gently onto the couch and presses a kiss to my forehead.

"Show me where it hurts"

He says, carefully taking my wrist into his big smooth palm.

"Braden, I think I'm supposed to do this. It's kind of my job."

I try to joke with him but he just shakes his head unamused. Sighing I show him with my finger.

"It hurts right here. I don't think anything is broken because nothing popped or cracked. It's probably just a sprain or a twist."

He nods and gets up to go get me some ice.

"I would have texted you earlier, but he kind of flipped a switch. I asked him if he still had feelings for me, and when I said I had moved on from him, he got really angry."

Braden sits back down in front of me on the coffee table and places the ice wrapped in a towel on my wrist.

"I'm so sorry baby. What he did was not okay."

I lean towards him and rest my head on his shoulder, savoring his delicious, comforting smell.

"I don't ever want to see him again. It was weird. It was almost like he wasn't even upset about his mom today. He just used it as an excuse to get me over to his place and try to get back with me."

Braden lovingly wraps his arms around my middle and places me onto his lap. I snuggle into the comfy sweatshirt he is wearing and focus on nursing my wrist.

"He is dangerous and unstable. I wish I stayed with you when you went in."

I shake my head.

"No, I feel like it would have escalated the situation even more. Thank you for being out front when I needed you."

He nods and snuggles into me, making sure to check on my wrist every couple minutes.

Beep

"Did you hear that?"

I ask. The beep was pretty faint, I can't really tell where it came from.

"What?"

Braden asks, looking around.

"Nothing."

I say pulling him back into me.

"When do you have work next?"

Braden asks me, brushing his hands through my hair.

"I have to close tonight. I think my shift starts at 2 pm. What time is it?"

He pulls out his phone to check the time. It reads 12pm.

"I need to go soon."

Beep

I ignore the beep. I feel like my mind is making it up.

I wish I didn't have to work and I could spend all my time with my boyfriend, but unfortunately, I have to make money somehow.

"Stay a little while longer?"

I nod. We stay wrapped up in each other's embrace for a while, waiting for my wrist to feel a little better.

——

It's almost the end of my shift and I feel like I am going crazy. Every two minutes I hear a Beep, and I cannot find where it is coming from. Thankfully, all I have to do is grab my stuff and I am out of here. I take my purse from the desk and check to make sure I have my keys, wallet, and phone. Sadly, we are short staffed again, so I am the only nurse to close and lock up the clinic tonight.

Beep

I swear I am losing it. I quickly turn off the clinic lights and close the door, making sure that everything is locked. Walking over to my car, I fish out my car keys from my purse and unlock the doors. I get in, close the door, put the keys into the ignition, and turn them.

Vgrrrrrr Vgrrrrrr

Really, my car has to die now? At 10 pm in a deserted creepy parking lot? I try the keys again a few more times, hoping my car starts, but nothing happens. Sighing, I get out of my car and pop the hood. Leaning over the engine, I try to figure out what is going on when all of a sudden, arms are wrapped around me and a cloth is pressed to my nose and mouth. Surprised, I breathe in and take in an overwhelmingly sweet smell coming from the cloth. I try to struggle out of the arms that are wrapped around me, but my body starts to go limp. The parking lot around me starts to blur and my eyes slowly close. The last thing I remember hearing is,

"We got her. Pretty easy to find her with that tracking device you put in her purse."

Chapter 17

I'm jolted awake by a ruthless slap to the face. My head pounds horribly as I slowly regain consciousness and open my stinging eyes. I try to rub them, but when I move my hands, I notice that I am tied tightly to a wooden chair with a disgusting tasting cloth stuffed into my mouth. Looking around, I take in my location. I'm sitting in the middle of a dark, dingy, smelly basement with concrete walls, ceilings, and light brown shag carpet. The air conditioner in the corner is blowing ridiculously loudly and there looks to be a dark red stain a few feet away from me on the floor. Hopefully, that isn't my blood.

"Lucy girl, are you awake?"

A familiar voice approaches from behind me and I tense up waiting for another slap. Kyle walks around to the front of me and bends down to my level.

"Ah, yes you are. You don't look too good."

I narrow my eyes angrily and try to wiggle out of the restraints I'm in. Of course, I don't look good, I was drugged, tied up, and now I've been slapped. I try to yell at him through the gross washcloth but all that comes out is muffled screaming.

"Don't be mad at me. I did this for us."

Kyle takes his finger and drags it across my face in a slow, sultry way. I try to move my head away but he grabs my chin roughly and pulls me towards him.

"Ever since we broke up a year ago, I've wanted you back. I followed you around for half a year. Sometimes watching you go to work, sometimes I would follow you home, and I got curious when you started visiting the prison. At that party, when you said you were visiting Braden every week, I knew I had to do something before he took you from me. So, I drugged your wine and tried to fuck you."

My heart stops and I reel back from his hand. He was the one that drugged me at the party?!

"You pushed me back and screamed so loud I had to leave before fuckin' Michelle found me. The next time I saw you, you were with that asshole Braden and I knew he claimed you just by the way he had his arm around you. It makes me sick how you can be with someone like him. You are MINE. Always have been and always will be. I did some deep research on Braden and found he was in the Cynicals. I reached out to them and they were more than happy to use you as bait to get Braden back."

Shaking my head I try once again to get out of my restraints. Kyle notices this and wraps his hand around my throat in a painfully crushing grip.

"STOP MOVING"

Immediately I stop fidgeting and he releases me. I let out a few coughs and try to regain a normal breathing pace. I can't believe what I'm hearing.

"Listen, once the Cynicals take Braden, you and I can be together. You'll realize how horrible he is and how much you want to be with me."

I narrow my eyes and shoot daggers at him. How dare he do this. This is not the Kyle I have known forever. What the hell has gotten into him?

"Settle down Kyle, we have shit to do. I can't listen to you yammer on and on all day."

A girl says from behind me. She walks around to stand next to Kyle and I recognize her to be the brunette, Sugar, that I saw sitting next to Braden at that bar. Sugar looks me up and down and slowly smirks deviously. Walking towards me, Sugar balls her fist and hits me right on the mouth in a painful blow. My head whips to the side and my lip splits open, blood spurting out.

"Let's rough her up so we can send a photo to Braden. Boss wants him over here as fast as possible. And keep her quiet, Boss doesn't know she's here."

Kyle nods and walks towards me. Bracing myself, I close my eyes knowing what's coming next.

"Lucy, this is all part of our plan. Endure the pain for our relationship."

Kyle brutally kicks my side and a sharp pain shoots across my ribs. I fall sideways onto the ground, still attached to the chair, and my face hits the concrete with a bang. My brain goes fuzzy for a few seconds, trying to stay conscious.

"This should be good enough. Smile Miss Lucy"

Sugar pulls out her phone from her back pocket and points it at me with a dangerous smirk. Snapping a photo of me, Sugar saves it to her phone.

"Let me call him actually, maybe we can get her to scream in the background."

Sugar presses a button on her device brings it up to her ear and leans casually against the closest wall.

Braden's POV

I lay awake in bed just staring at my phone. After we saw Sugar at the bar, I have been making Lucy text me as soon as she gets home from work, especially if she has the night shift. I would offer to drive her but I don't have my car. I could drop her off and pick her up with her car, but if something happens at work, I would want Lucy to have her car with her to escape. Even though I hate this texting option, it's the safest way.

I look at the clock again and realize that it's now 11 pm and Lucy still has not texted that she made it home safe. Deciding to not take any chances, I get out of bed and pull on the black jeans I was wearing earlier. Tucking my phone in my back pocket, I make my way out of my apartment and up one floor to where Lucy, Michelle, and Kiera live. Hopefully, Lucy just forgot to text me and she is safe, sound, and asleep.

Knocking on the door anxiously, I wait for one of the girls to answer. A few seconds later, a sleepy Michelle pulls open the door.

"Braden?"

I look past Michelle in the apartment and scan the area for Lucy.

"Hey, sorry to wake you but is Lucy here? She hasn't texted me that she made it home safe."

Michelle's eyes go wide and she steps aside to let me into the apartment.

"I thought she was with you. She slept over last night, I assumed she would sleep over there again tonight!"

My heart skips a beat and I barge into Lucy's closed room. Her room is empty and so is her bathroom.

"Shit."

I say anxiously.

"She is usually home by now. Where could she be?"

Michelle says, running her hands through her braids.

"What's going on?"

Kiera says annoyed, coming out of her and Michelle's room in her pajamas.

"Lucy hasn't made it home yet and her shift ended an hour ago."

I say frustrated to Kiera. I take a few deep breaths and pull out my phone to call her.

"Maybe she stopped for food or something?"

Kiera says hopefully while wrapping her arms around Michelle. Pressing her name in my contacts, I wait for her to pick up. After a few rings, her phone goes to voicemail. I try once more and it goes to voicemail again.

"She always picks up."

Michelle says nervously. A surge of anger flows through me and I lean against the wall trying to calm myself down. If they touch her, I'll kill them. A buzzing comes from my pocket and I look to see who it is quickly, hoping it's Lucy.

"Is it her?!"

Kiera asks, coming over to my side to look who it is.

"It's an unknown number."

I say. Pressing the accept button, I put my phone up to my ear.

"Hello?"

I say slowly, trying to hold back my anger. I recognize the sickly sweet voice as soon as I hear it.

"Braden! So nice of you to pick up."

I tense and hold myself back from crushing my phone in my hand.

"What the hell do you want, Sugar?"

I hear her disgusting, high-pitched laugh from the other side of the line and I ball my fist.

"You know why I'm calling right? I have her."

My suspicions are confirmed. Angrily I tighten my fist and punch the wall to let out some aggression. I need to think clearly, come up with a plan to get Lucy out of this.

"Don't you dare touch her. Let her go right now."

Sugar once again laughs through the line.

"Why would I do that? She is pretty fun if I do say so myself. Kyle was right, she is quite a gem."

My feelings of anger halt for a second while I take in what Sugar just said.

"What do you mean Kyle?"

"Oh, Kyle helped us grab little Lucy. He put a tracking device in her purse and gave us her location all for a chance to be with her again."

I knew that preppy asshole was trouble. The next time I see him, he's dead. I make eye contact with Michelle and Kiera and grit my teeth furiously.

"What do you want Sugar?"

"Boss wants you here to talk. Come to the address I will send you alone and unarmed. Do this and your precious Lucy won't be hurt any more than she already is."

"WHAT THE FUCK DO YOU MEAN 'ANY MORE THAN SHE ALREADY IS'!"

I yell into the phone. I am on the edge of destroying everything in this room out of rage.

"I'll send you a photo of her. She might need some stitches on that lip of hers."

I receive a photo of my Lucy tied to a chair, on the ground, with a busted lip, and bruises forming on her body.

"Don't touch her."

I threaten lowly.

"If you follow my directions, nothing else will happen to her."

Sugar hangs up abruptly and I take a few seconds to violently stare at the screen of my phone. I receive a text from Sugar containing an address to a house in the sketchy part of Seattle.

"You can't go alone. It's too dangerous."

Michelle says seriously. Kiera nods in agreement while taking a step towards the door.

"You heard Sugar. If you come with me, Lucy gets hurt. Stay here and make sure we have enough first aid supplies for her."

Michelle and Kiera take a nervous look at each other and nod towards me.

"Call us if anything happens. We will be there as soon as possible."

I nod my head at them and quickly head out the door to the address.

Lucy's POV

I am still laying on the floor in a foggy state when I hear Sugar hang up on Braden. I know he's coming for me, but I need to find a way to get out of here before he arrives. Discreetly, I again try to loosen the restraints that are tying my hands together behind the chair. In this lying-down position, I have a little more leverage to get out of the ties. Suddenly, I hear loud footsteps coming down the stairs and I stop loosening the ties.

"Shit, Boss is coming. Get her up."

Sugar says nervously and orders Kyle. He walks over to me, grabs my sensitive arms, and jerks me and the chair back into a sitting position. I can barely keep my head up. It's pounding so painfully.

"What's going on down here?"

A deep voice booms from behind me. I think that I recognize the voice for a second but forget about it because my brain can't focus.

"Deathface, this is the bait to get Braden here. His random little girlfriend he somehow cares about."

Sugar says while crossing her arms and leaning against the concrete wall. Loud, stomping footsteps move from behind my back to stand right in front of me. Mustering up the strength that I have left, I raise my head to look at the man standing in front of me. As soon as we make eye contact, my heart stops in shock.

"Dave?"

My brother's eyes widen and we stay there staring at each other in surprise. How the hell?

Thanks for reading! In the next ten-ish chapters I will be starting to wrap up the story. I know generally what I want to happen, but if anyone has something they would like to see between Braden and Lucy,(ex. an idea for a smut scene, a date idea, etc.), let me know and I will definitely consider it! Have a great week everyone <3

Chapter 18

"Lucy, what the fuck are you doing here."

Dave says dumbfoundedly. He stays there for a couple of seconds staring numbly at me until something snaps in him and he yells out.

"Sugar. Kyle? What the hell...... , Get these fucking ties off my goddamn sister. Why did you bring her here?"

Dave yells angrily at Sugar and Kyle. Both of them jump in surprise and immediately start untying my hands and feet. I wince in pain as they brush against some of the bruises around the ties. My brother notices and starts to become angry red. As soon as I am untied, he securely picks me up in his arms and marches us up the stairs. My head is spinning and all I can do is simply lay my head against Dave's stiff shoulder. He pushes open a door and lays me down gently on a couch.

"Lucy, drink this."

Dave hands me a cup of water and I down it, hoping that it will help my concussion. As I drink, Dave pulls out a first aid kit, cleans the wound on my face, and applies some gel on the visible bruises located on my leg and arms. When I finish the water, he sets the cup down for me and applies some soothing cream to my busted lip.

"Why are you here? How did you find me?"

Dave asks gently, but I can tell he is holding back frustration. I shake my head.

"Give me five minutes, I feel like I'm going to throw up."

I respond, sitting up on the couch and resting my head in my hands. He moves to sit next to me and gently rubs my back.

"Answer me this. Are Sugar and Kyle the ones that did this to you?"

Without looking him in the eyes, I nod my head yes.

"I've never seen Kyle around here. I have no idea what he is doing helping Sugar. I'm going to fuck them up for this."

Dave grunts angrily and gets up from the couch.

"I'll be back in ten minutes. Stay here and focus on your breathing."

Before I know it, Dave storms out of the office and locks the door. I faintly hear yelling and grunts of pain from down the stairs but I do as Dave says and I focus on my breathing. Even though my head is spinning, my lip is busted, and my ribcage is burning, I have to talk to my brother. I haven't seen him in two years. A few minutes later, Dave unlocks the door and walks back into the office, not being phased by the obvious beating he just did. He takes a seat next to me and looks me in the eye. I beat him to the chase and ask a question first.

"You're the boss? The boss of the Cynicals? Since when? I thought you were in fucking Florida? How?"

Dave sighs and leans back on the couch.

"I never wanted you to be in this part of my life, Lucy. I became a member of the Cynicals when I was fifteen and worked up in the ranks. You knew we barely scraped by paying the bills growing up. The Cynicals offered me money, and I took it for our family."

Since he was fifteen? This has been going on since I was twelve and I never knew?

"Dave, I thought you were on the boxing team?! But you were in a GANG? Why didn't you tell me? Was that why you always came home busted up? Did mom and dad know?"

He avoids eye contact with me and defensively crosses his arms.

"Lucy, you are my baby sister. I never wanted you to get involved or be at risk, I still don't. And, yes, mom and dad knew. They tried to convince me to stop but they didn't get it. This gang is my job. It's a part of my life, you can't get out of it."

I frown at him.

"That's not true. You said you moved to Florida. Obviously, you got away from it while being there for a while."

I see him visibly swallow and make apologizing eye contact with me.

"I never moved to Florida, Lucy. I was always here."

I take that in for a few seconds. He was always here. Just a few miles away from my broken, grieving, lonely heart, and didn't tell me. I stare at him blankly.

"Lucy, I know it was wrong. But I couldn't deal. I had so many things on my plate, it was easier to get away from everything and dive into my work than deal with the grief. I always thought about you though. Those voicemails you leave or left, they are the highlight of my month."

I stand up angrily, not believing what I'm hearing. My eyesight blurs painfully for a second but I push through.

"WHAT THE HELL DO YOU MEAN YOU WERE HERE THE WHOLE TIME? You left me alone, broken, devastated after our parent's death and you didn't even think to call? I don't care that you thought about me or listened to my voicemail or how it was your way of dealing with things. You are my older brother and I needed you. How could you?!"

Dave stands up angrily and cowers over me.

"Look, I'm sorry, okay! I needed space. I know I should have been there for you and I regret not supporting you after. I didn't want to drag you into this shit because it's dangerous. If I grieved with you after, we would have gotten closer and more involved in each other's lives. People watch me, Lucy. You would have been used as bait."

"Well look here dumbass! I've just been used as bait for Braden. Even you going away didn't stop this from happening. I wish you were in my life after mom and dad. How is that too much to ask?"

Dave clenches his jaw and looks down away from me to think for a few seconds. He sighs, relaxes, and walks around the room for a couple of minutes, seeming to gather his thoughts. Finally, he turns to me.

"We can't change what's happened. Sugar and Kyle have told the whole gang about you being my sister and Braden's lover, which we are fucking talking about later. You're part of this now whether I like it or not."

My breathing starts to quicken at this realization and I sit back down on the couch to catch my breath.

"And I'm going to prove to you going forward that you can trust me. That I can be there for you and protect you as your older brother."

I shake my head and wrap my arms around myself.

"I don't want any part of your gang. I just want to be with Braden, have you in my life, and go home."

Dave walks over to me and brings me into a comforting hug. I stay stiff as a board, not being able to comprehend the idea that my brother is hugging me. How can I trust him when he abandoned me.

"Lucy, you're known to be important to two gang members. Our rivals will target you. It's a complicated mess now. You have to trust me."

"I don't know if I can"

I whisper sadly. Dave pulls back from our hug and frowns.

"Can you try, at the very least, for your safety?"

I think for a minute, weighing my very limited options. I slowly nod. Letting out a tight breath, Dave moves on to a different topic.

"Next thing. Why the hell are you dating Braden?"

I furrow my eyebrows. He switched up moods real quick. My head is pounding too hard to deal with the protective brother act today.

"Save it, Dave. I love him and there's nothing you can do about it."

He gets up from the couch and leans on his desk in the center of the room with a glare plastered across his face.

"Love him!? How did you even meet him? The last time I checked he was still in prison and I was waiting for him to get out and join again. I swear to God Lucy if you tell me you were in prison....."

I roll my eyes.

"No! I was his prison pen pal, that's how we met. I've never been arrested."

Dave drops his mouth open in surprise.

"YOU HAD A PRISON PEN PAL? AND YOU FELL IN LOVE WITH HIM? Lucy that is the stupidest most dangerous thing -"

I furiously stand up and cover his mouth with my hand.

"How dare you criticize my life and who I love when you weren't even fucking there. You should be thanking Braden that he was there for me and supported me while you were neglecting our sibling relationship. I'm done. If you're going to yell at me about the choice I made in the life you refused to be in, I'm leaving."

Dave gets surprisingly quiet. Moving my hand away, I take a couple of angry steps back waiting for his response. After a few seconds, Dave crosses his arms and avoids eye contact. It seems like this is his go-to move when he doesn't want to admit something.

"Fine. You're right. I shouldn't be criticizing you, even if your choices weren't the safest. I wasn't there. But I feel like I can still be mad at him for dragging you into this."

Rubbing my temples, I relax my painful headache.

"You can feel whatever you want to feel. Just don't criticize me."

Dave, annoyed, nods at me and I drop it. Suddenly, an intercom rings out

Agent has arrived. Heading upstairs. He is not armed.

I make confused eye contact with my brother.

"Looks like your boyfriend has arrived."

"Agent?"

Dave shrugs.

"My name is Deathface because I'm the face of this deadly gang. He is Agent because he's our secret agent, our spy. It's safer to hide our identities."

I nod, still a little confused, and turn towards the door waiting for Braden to come in, assuming he is coming to the office. A few seconds later, he barges in, fists up, preparing for a fight. He scans around the room looking for something. As soon as we make eye contact, he rushes over to me and stands protectively in front of me.

"Deathface. If you wanted to talk to me so badly you could have just ambushed me instead of using Sugar and that ass Kyle to bring my girl into it."

Braden reaches behind to gently wrap his hand around mine. Butterflies erupt in my stomach and a feeling of safety washes over me.

My brother crosses his arms putting on an intimidating front, and sits down in the chair behind his desk.

"If you think for one second that I would hurt my own sister like that, you know nothing about me after our ten years of friendship."

Every muscle in Braden's body stiffens. He tightens his hold on my hand and turns to me. Raking his eyes down my body and taking in every injury, he swallows and connects our gazes.

"You're his sister?"

I nod.

"I kept her out of all this shit until you came along, Agent."

Braden grits his teeth and turns back to Dave.

"At least I was honest with her, and I could care less about what you think, Deathface. You got me thrown in jail."

Braden seethes. Dave stands up angrily and storms over to where Braden and I are standing.

"I was not behind that. Gunner and Throatcut disobeyed orders. I kicked them out and sent them on a dead-end mission to get arrested after they named you."

"Oh shut up. You knew I wanted to leave and was hiding out avoiding you. Even if you weren't behind my arrest, you wouldn't let me go."

"Ten years Agent. For ten years you were our spy, of course, I didn't let you go. Do you think I'm crazy?! I wanted to meet with you to initiate you back. You're part of this Agent"

Dave slams his fist down on the table and I intervene.

"Calm down. Dave, I know you want Braden back, but please. Let us go."

I feel a warmth in my nose but I ignore it.

"I don't want back in, Deathface. There's nothing you can do to change that."

Dave shakes his head and rounds the desk.

"You don't understand. The Killers, there up to no good. They got a new member. He's a special engineer and he is making a special kind of cocaine that is poison. They are planning on releasing it onto Seattle as an act of power. Do you know how many people are going to die?"

Both Braden and I still.

"Who are the Killers?"

I ask nervously. Braden turns to me and wraps one of his arms around me to support my body weight. I think he can tell I'm getting weaker by the minute.

"Our rival gang. I worked as a spy for the Cynicals, watching them. I knew they wanted to attack the public to show their power, but I never knew how big they would go."

Suddenly a trickle of blood rushes out of my nose and I become extremely lightheaded.

"Shit. I need to take her home. Your stupid ass members did this to her."

Braden leans me back onto the couch and takes the towel that Dave hands to him and presses it against my nose.

"Oh, believe me, they aren't members anymore. It's going to take a while for them to recover and be anything for a while."

Braden angrily nods and smooths my hair back.

"Take her home. I'll send a few members after you to guard the area."

Braden turns around and seethes.

"We don't need anything from your members. They've already done enough."

Dave places an angry, dominant hand on Braden's shoulder.

"I don't care what you want. That's my baby sister and I'm not sending her out of here without protection. In case you haven't figured this out yet, the Killers have now seen her with you and probably know that she's my sister. I found Sugar texting everyone she knew about Lucy before I got to her. You need backup."

Braden scowls in annoyance and turns back to me. I can barely register what's going on at this point, my concussion is fuzzing up my brain.

"Take her home, and we will talk tomorrow. Text me updates about her. I know you still have my number Agent."

Braden reluctantly and worriedly nods his head. He bends down to pick me up and carry me bridal style. I wrap my limp arms around his neck, lean my pounding head against him, and blackout.

Sorry to leave you guys on a cliffhanger last week, hopefully, you could see all the pieces fall into place during this chapter. I know this chapter was a little heavier than normal, but it's a turning point for the book. In the next chapter, I promise there will be a little bit more fluff if you like that type of writing. Let me know if anything in this chapter did not make sense and I will make sure to clarify it in the next one. P.S. all your comments are so funny I love them. See you next week <3

Chapter 19

I wake up to a light caress of my hair and the warm feeling of blankets covering me. Even though my head feels like it weighs a thousand pounds and my body is sore, I open my eyes to the glowing light. I make eye contact with Braden's worried eyes from where he is laying next to me on my bed. He continues to gently brush through my hair with his fingers, and occasionally run his thumb along my cheek.

"How are you feeling?"

Braden murmurs nervously. I can tell he is worried about me from the number of medical supplies stacked up on my nightstand and the tension in his shoulders. Reaching up, I wrap my arm around his shoulders and bring him into a loving hug.

"I'm feeling okay. Still a little confused but I'm glad to be home with you."

Braden nods into my shoulder.

"What time is it? Did I miss work?"

Braden shakes his head.

"No, I called your work letting them know that you will be out for a few days resting up. Hope that was okay."

I nod and reassure him.

"That's fine, thank you for doing that."

"Where does it hurt? I have some bruise cream I need to put on you."

I uncurl myself from his embrace and slowly sit up on the bed against the propped-up pillows.

"Ummm, mostly my stomach area. My head hurts a little too but I think if I drink a lot of water I will be fine."

While reaching over to the nightstand to grab some cream, Braden sighs and shakes his head.

"This is all my fault. I should have been more careful, I should have known they would go after you."

"Hey. Stop."

I firmly place my hand on his strong bicep and he tenses.

"It's not your fault. It's Kyle and Sugar's fault I got wrapped up in this. We will figure this out. We are in this together now."

Frustrated, Braden sits on the bed with his legs hanging off and turns to me.

"No. I don't want you in this mess. It's mine and your brother's shit to figure out. I want you to rest and heal up."

I roll my eyes and try to reach for the bruise cream in his hands but he pulls it away from me.

"I'm serious Lucy. I don't want you to be involved in this."

"Braden, it's my brother and my boyfriend that is not only butting heads but also trying to save all of Seattle. I'm going to help and there is nothing you can do about that."

Now Braden rolls his eyes and screws open the bottle of cream.

"Let's talk about this later baby. Will you promise me that at least you will focus on feeling better?"

I sigh. This conversation is not over but I'm not in the mood to bicker.

"Fine. Are you going to put that cream on me or just stare at me all worried?"

Braden giggles and presses a kiss on my cheek. Slowly he reaches down and pulls my shirt off my body leaving me in just my bra. Braden continues to place sensual kisses down my neck, over my perky breasts and landing over the bruise that is sitting on my stomach. My breath catches when Braden reaches up with his hands and pulls my thighs apart so he can rest in between them. A low moan slips out of my mouth when he gently rubs the warm cream on top of the purple area on my stomach. Braden places another kiss behind my ear and I feel him smile against my skin.

"Now that I think about it, I think I have another place that you can rub that cream on."

I whisper in his ear. Braden laughs and pulls back from me.

"As much as I would love to make love to you right now, I don't think a lot of fast movements for you would be a good idea."

He places a chaste kiss on my cheek and stands up from the bed. Stretching his arms above his head, the bottom of his shirt rises to expose the toned v lines of his stomach. Groaning, I reach over, grab the pillow sitting next to me, and cover my eyes.

"Not fair! You can't tempt me with that move right after getting me all worked up!"

I hear another victorious round of laughter and Braden walks into the kitchen. The rest of the morning is filled with cuddles, gentle kisses, and a lot of naps. Braden is kind enough to make me grilled cheese for lunch and serve it to me in bed. Resting the tray in front of me, he climbs under the covers next to me and reaches for his sandwich.

"Thank you, baby. You are the sweetest to me."

I lean over and steal a kiss from him before we dig into the grilled cheeses.

"Hey, are Kiera and Michelle doing okay? Hopefully, they weren't too freaked out when I didn't come home."

Braden shifts uncomfortably, obviously not liking to talk about that scary moment.

"Yeah, they were pretty scared but they are at work now. I was nervous you didn't text me that made it home safe, so I came up to your apartment to check on things. Michelle opened the door. As soon as I asked about you, she flipped. Kiera came rushing in and got nervous too."

I reach over and hold his hand, squeezing it reassuringly.

"I remember being so scared and angry at the same time. I got a call from Sugar telling me to meet her at the warehouse and before I could think straight I was rushing over there. Michelle and Kiera begged me to let them come but I couldn't risk Sugar hurting you anymore and putting them in danger."

"You did a great job. If you were in danger I honestly don't know what I would do except for freak out and tear apart the world to get you home. And, I was fine. Dave saved me before they could cause any deep damage."

Braden leans his forehead against our held hands and lets out a breath.

"Thanks, baby. It's weird having someone I want to watch out for other than myself. I know that sounds selfish but I've never really had another person in my life that I would do anything for."

My heart cracks a little bit hearing that. Shaking my head, I caress his jaw so he looks at me.

"I love being there for you Braden, and I want to continue being there for you. So get used to it, I'm not going anywhere."

Braden smiles lovingly at me, genuinely conveying the thanks he has for our relationship. I pick up my grilled cheese and cheers his sandwich that is resting in his other hand. We eat in comfortable silence for a little while, watching family feud reruns on the small television across from my bed.

"Hey, baby?"

"Hmmm"

I absentmindedly answer.

"You're a little stinky."

I let out a lighthearted laugh, roll my eyes, and bat his shoulder.

"Well excuse me for not being able to walk to the shower without crying out in pain."

Braden smiles at me and gets up from the bed. He walks around to the other side, bends down, and loops his arms under me in a gentle way. Picking me up, Braden carries me over to the bathroom.

"Guess we are taking a shower together!"

Heat blooms on my face as I remember what happened last time we showered together. My arousal from earlier resumes as soon as images from a few nights ago and his defined v-line pop into my head. Braden sets me down on top of the counter and swiftly takes my bra off, leaving my bare breasts on display. He watches them bounce from the bra a few times and clenches his jaw in restraint. Maybe I can convince him to repeat our last showering experience. Braden shakes his head and slips my sweatpants and underwear off my body. As he does this, I reach up and pull his shirt off his body. I hold back a grimace when I stretch my arms above my head and ignore it. Once I am fully naked and sitting on the counter, Braden smoothly takes off his pants, leaving his full manhood on display for me. I notice that he is semi-erect, so without thinking, I reach my hand forward. Suddenly, Braden bats my hand away from him and picks me up, and places me into the shower.

"No monkeying around baby."

I lean my weight against him as he turns on the warm water and rests his hand on my ass. We spend a couple of minutes just hugging each other under the running water. I press a few kisses to his chest and reach for the body wash. I squirt a little into my hands, rub them together and start massaging Braden's chest and arms. He closes his eyes, obviously loving the feeling of the warm bubbles over his skin. Grabbing the shampoo, I also put a little into my hands and lather it up. When I reach up to rub it in his thick hair, a sharp pain radiates through my side and I let out a wince. Braden's eyes pop open and he stops my hands, scraping the soap from them, and rubbing it into his hair.

"I got it."

He says. I nod. Once he is done thoroughly rubbing his hair, he moves onto mine. I close my eyes, enjoying the feeling of his fingers massaging my scalp with shampoo and conditioner, gently pulling on my strands.

"Let's rinse this out."

I open my eyes and let him move me under the clean, warm water. As he is doing this I admire his beautiful face, his strong nose, his chiseled jawline, and delicious full lips. This man is so kind to me. He makes eye contact with me and the world stops.

"I love you."

I whisper. He smiles and my heart bursts with warmth and love.

"I love you too."

We finish rinsing all the soap off our bodies and then get out together. I dry myself off with the fluffy white towel that is hanging on the rack but ask for help drying my legs as I don't want to bend down. After giving Braden a thank you smooch, I turn on the fan and walk to my closet in the bedroom. When I have one foot into my sweatpants, my phone rings loudly from the bed.

"Baby, will you get that? It's right there."

Braden nods and picks up the phone.

"Hello?"

A few seconds pass by and Braden angrily frowns.

"Deathface, I told you to leave her the fuck alone."

"Hey! Is that my brother?"

I walk quickly over to him and snatch the phone out of his hand. Braden grumbles angrily and sits down on the bed, pulling my body onto his lap.

"Dave?"

"Hey, how are you feeling?"

I swallow and sigh. It's so weird to suddenly have him back in my life. I know this is what I've wanted for the longest time, but now that he is here and has dangerous ties, I am unsure how to feel.

"A little sore, but I'll be fine in a few days. Did you need something?"

I hear some moving about on the other side of the line, almost like he is getting somewhere private.

"I've been thinking about your situation. I think I have a deal that I can make with you and Braden where I can grant him freedom from the gang, as well as get done what I need him to do."

I roll my eyes and make annoyed eye contact with Braden.

"I don't understand why you just can't let him go. He doesn't want to be in the gang anymore and you should want that too. Without him being tangled in dangerous missions, I will be less in danger."

I hear him grumble frustrated on the other end.

"You don't get it, Lucy. The whole gang is watching me. If I let Braden just walk away, other members will think they can get away with it too. I want you to be safe, but there is a certain way of doing things."

Braden clenches his jaw and takes the phone out of my hand.

"Deathface, I will meet with you. Where."

I reach over and put the phone on speaker.

"I'm coming too."

Immediately, both of them gasp angrily and yell,

"No way."

I knew they would react like this.

"I'm going to be involved either way. If Braden does this, I will be in danger just by being associated with both of you. Might as well make myself useful."

I run my hands through Braden's damp hair calmly, trying to persuade him with some loving touch. My brother is quiet for a few seconds, almost like he is thinking. Defeatedly, Dave agrees.

"I don't like this idea."

Braden complains while pulling me in closer to his warm, half-naked body.

"I know, but there's no way I'm leaving you both alone in this."

"Let's meet in a week to talk, I'll send you a location soon. In the meantime, Lucy, rest up."

I nod, determined.

"I promise, Dave."

Braden ends the call and rests his head into my chest nervously.

"If something else happens to you, I don't know what I'm going to do."

I place a comforting kiss on the top of his head and rub his back lovingly. I know he wants to protect me but there is no way I'm sitting on the sidelines for this one.

"I promise, everything will be okay."

Sorry for no update last week, I had midterms! Send some positive vibes out in the atmosphere for my midterm grades! :) <3 This chapter had a little bit more fluff than usual, but who doesn't love some fluff. ;)

Chapter 20

The darkness outside is adding to the ominous vibe of tonight as Braden and I drive to Manny's, a dive bar in Seattle. Dave texted Braden this bar as the location to meet tonight, saying it is most safe and inconspicuous to meet in public. Dave mentioned something about not being able to fully trust his gang right now, so meeting together in public instead of at the house is the best option. After what Sugar did to me, I think he is being extra careful.

I glance over at Braden, who is in the driver's seat and focused on the road. The warmth of his palm on my thigh sends butterflies to my stomach, making me rake my eyes down his handsome figure. Right now I can't see much of him though as we were told to dress in disguise. Braden is dressed in an extremely baggy sweatshirt that's hood is pulled up and over a ball cap that hides his face. He is also wearing oversized black sweats and high-top Nikes. As for me, I treated this as more of a Halloween costume opportunity.

My hair is tucked under a chin-length red wig, and I am also wearing circular glasses, an orange puffy vest, and a black skirt. I am channeling Velma tonight, trying to get to the bottom of this mystery.

"Why are you looking at me like that?"

Braden whispers huskily, not taking his intense gaze off the road. I swallow and trace his sharp jawline with my eyes.

"Like what?"

I ask, pretending to be oblivious. He chuckles slowly and cracks a smirk.

"I didn't know sweatpants and a sweatshirt turned you on so much babe."

Braden looks over at me and pointedly looks down at my crossed legs. I blush, embarrassed, not even realizing that I crossed my legs to cope with my slight wetness.

"Sorry, I must be in a mood or something today."

I say, turning my head and looking out the window, noticing that we are pulling into the parking lot. Braden pulls into a spot, turns off the ignition, and grasps my chin, turning my head towards him.

"I'm feeling it too. But, it might just be because of how sexy you look in that wig or how tight that little skirt is."

I feel him tighten his hand on my thigh and lean into my right ear. I let out a small breathy moan.

"Or it's because I haven't been able to touch you for a week now. Thankfully, tonight I think you're up for it, huh?"

Breathlessly, I nod and close my eyes at the intoxicating feeling of his breath hitting my ear.

"And when I fuck you tonight, I want you to keep the wig and that little skirt on. How does that sound, baby?"

I let out a moan when he moves his strong, rough hand down my neck, tightens it, and runs his hot, wet tongue along the spot under my ear. Just as soon as he started though, he takes his hands off me, hops out of the car, opens up my door for me, and reaches out his hand nonchalantly.

"Ready to go? We can't be late."

I roll my eyes and take his hand, annoyed at him for getting me all hot and bothered without acting on anything.

"Bastard."

I mumble under my breath. Braden laughs sinisterly, opens the door to Manny's, and guides me inside. The bar is a normal dive bar, with bottles hanging on the wall, multiple beers on tap, people at tables as well as standing at the bar, dirty-looking lights, and the smell of peanuts. Braden points to a dimly lit booth in the back corner where my brother and a woman with black and purple hair are sitting. I follow behind Braden, holding his hand tightly, as we make our way to the booth. Dave stands up from the booth and embraces me into a warm and protective hug.

"Hey, you."

"Hey, Dave."

Dave steps back and gestures to the girl with purple hair standing next to him.

"Lucy, this is Missy. She is just a few years older than you and is in the gang with me. She is pretty high up and I trust her with my life."

I smile at Missy and she pulls me into a hug that is bone-crushing but feels like sunshine at the same time.

"So nice to finally meet you. After seeing years of Deathface moping around missing you, it is great to finally have you here and in our lives. I know the circumstances that brought you into this were not great, but you are here, and I'm glad to meet you."

My heart warms and I hug her back gently.

"It's nice to meet you too Missy."

Out of the corner of my eye, I see Dave and Braden nod coldly at each other before they sit down in the booth. Missy and I follow suit, sitting down and scooching over. Four beers are set on the table, one for each of us. I notice that Missy and Dave sit as close together as Braden and I do, except they don't hold hands or show any PDA. Interesting.

"Thank you for meeting us here. After the Sugar fiasco, I didn't want to chance meeting in the house until things died down. Nice disguise, Lucy."

I nod and lean back in the booth, getting more comfortable.

"I know Agent, you don't want to be in this gang anymore. It's not a family anymore to you and I get that. But, I can't just let you go. Especially after how Sugar acted out, I need to be as strict as possible. So, I have come up with a compromise. You help us stop the Killers from killing thousands of people with laced cocaine, and I'll let you go. The only time I'll see you is when I see Lucy."

Braden crosses his arms for a minute, thinking.

"What would you need from me."

Deathface smirks victoriously.

"The same thing I always need, for you to get information. Your friend, Clide, has been in contact with the Killers recently. I've seen Snake go into that steakhouse of his a few times, looking suspicious."

Braden nods and licks his lips.

"Who's Snake? Why do we need information on him?"

"Snake is the head of the Killers. He is fucked up in the head, always doing dangerous shit, I don't want you near him, Lucy."

Deathface explains and leans over the table. Braden adamantly nods in agreement before taking a sip of his beer.

"I still want to be in this and help. I can't just sit around and wait while thousands of people are in danger."

Dave rolls his eyes and looks over at Missy who is giving him a harsh, convincing glare.

"Fine. You can help out Missy. She figures out important logistics, makes detailed plans, and doesn't get involved in the violence. You want to help? Help her."

Braden nods from the side of me.

"Good idea, Deathface. Lucy, help Missy."

From across the table, Missy cracks a smile at me. I can see in her eyes there is mischievous trouble brewing.

"Braden, I need information on Wednesday, which is in two days. Talk to Clide by then. As for you Miss Lucy, meet me at my apartment on Wednesday night. We will go over the information found and create a plan."

Dave and Missy stand up from the booth slowly, and both hug me.

"If either of you run into trouble, call me. Braden, keep my sister safe."
Braden shakes Dave's hand, warming up to him after they have come to a compromise. Dave and Missy turn and walk out the door, their hands almost close enough to touch, but they never do.

"How do you feel about all this?"

I ask, shifting to face Braden. He reaches down to the table, takes his last sip of beer, and takes a breath.

"I don't like you being involved in this mess but the compromise he made is good. One more mission and then I'm done. Back in the day, I would have died for this proposition. Now, I have greater stakes so it's nerve-racking."

Squeezing his hand, I also finish the last of my beer, loving the taste of the amber liquid. We stayed a bit longer at the bar, watching the basketball game play on the big screen, and talking to the bartender who got me another beer.

"Can we go home soon? It's getting late."

Braden looks down at his watch, notices that it is already 10 pm, and nods at me. Sliding off the barstool, I make eye contact with the bartender, flagging her down. Before Braden notices, I give her my card and sign the check.

"Hey! Did you just pay?"

Braden questions me, annoyed. I put my card back into my purse and grab his hand.

"Maybe..."

I say teasingly. Braden narrows his eyes at me and starts walking us both towards the door.

"You know I don't mind paying, Lucy. It makes me feel like I'm mooching off you when you pay."

Braden opens my car door for me, gesturing me to get in. I instead wrap my arms around him and place a soft kiss on his cheek.

"You aren't mooching off me, I promise. But, I think you know how you can pay me back tonight."

Pulling away, I meet his intense stare and give him a wink before sitting in the car. The drive home is filled with sexual tension, it is hard to breathe. We make searing eye contact several times, brush our hands against each other in anticipation, and I even catch him adjusting himself in his seat at a red light. Finally, we park in the parking lot. Holding hands, we walk through the lobby, heading up to his apartment.

Immediately, when the apartment door is opened, Braden's lips are on me. They are soft and rough at the same time, leading me to moan into his mouth. Taking the opportunity, he swipes his tongue into my mouth, tasting me and scraping up against my teeth and tongue. I slowly trail my hands down his heaving chest, scratching my fingernails above the band of his loose sweatpants. We walk back together, bumping and falling onto the couch clumsily. I have to hold a laugh back when Braden almost falls off the side of it when he tries to lay on top of me. Raking my hands under his sweatshirt, I gently pull it off and discard it to the side. Braden pulls back from kissing me to remove his sweatshirt, and slowly unzip my puffy vest. He throws it to the side and rips off my mock neck sweater feverishly. I gasp as he moves my bra to the side, presses a wet kiss to one of my nipples, and massages the other roughly.

"Yesss"

I moan out, enjoying the feeling of his hot mouth on my breasts. Reaching down, I pull down his sweatpants, reach into his boxers, and pump him from base to tip, loving the soft steel in my hand. Braden jerks in surprise, but moans under my touch. Reaching behind me, he unclasps my bra and throws it to the ground. He continues to bite and suck my breasts, making sure each one has equal attention. Wanting friction on my core, I take my hand off his length, reach around to the back of his hips, press him into me and grind myself against his now naked hardness. Noticing my need, Braden moves downwards towards my core, flips up my skirt, and pushes my underwear to the side.

He dives down in between my legs and swirls his rough tongue against my center at a deliciously fast pace. Sucking harshly on my bud, he pushes two fingers inside of me, stretching my wet core. I buck and moan out at the pleasurable intrusion. He pumps those fingers in and out of me, torturously slow, but flicks my clit with his tongue. Wriggling underneath him, I feel a fire in my core starting to build. Before it builds any farther, he detaches himself from my pussy, turns me around so my ass is in the air, and pulls on the wig still attached to my head so my back is arched.

"This wig and skirt are so sexy, my love. I need to be inside you."

Braden rips the panties off my body and moves my skirt to the side so my wet core is exposed. He reaches into his wallet resting in the pocket of his sweats, pulls out a condom, sexily rips it open with his teeth, and rolls it onto himself.

"Are you ready?"

Braden asks me, sweetly checking for consent. I nod my head yes and he thrusts into my pussy, filling me up fully. I spread my legs apart further giving him more space to enter me and adjust to the large size of me. Braden thrusts in and out of me at an increasingly fast and strong pace, making me moan out. I bite my lip to stop myself from screaming as he continues to hit my g spot with his thick length. He tightens the grip he has on my shoulder-length red hair and makes me arch my back even more. Reaching forward, I dig my nails into the arm of the couch to try to stay grounded as he is ramming into me from behind. Braden starts to circle my clit with his fingers, sending shockwaves through my body. I squeeze my pussy around his length a few times which makes him groan huskily.

"Please, please."

I beg and whimper.

"What? Do you need to come, baby?"

I nod desperately, causing him to smirk behind me at pick up his pace, thrusting in and

out of me aggressively. My vision blurs for a second making me breathless and tremble under his hands and length.

"Come for me, Lucy."

I try to scream as I reach my peak, but Braden's hand comes around to cover my mouth. Grunting and moaning out, Braden collapses on top of me, smushing me into the couch, still in me from behind. Both of us take a few seconds to calm down and recenter ourselves after coming. Soon, Braden slowly pulls out of me and discards the dirty condom in the trash. Laying back down on the couch, he pulls me into his arms and we take some quiet moments in each other's arms. I notice though, that my wig is no longer on my head. Peeking up from his shoulder, I look around, and spot it on the floor. Before I have a chance to grab it, Braden reaches down and grabs it.

"I think I might want to keep this."

Braden says with a joking smirk. I laugh and roll my eyes at him, burying myself back into his warm and comfortable shoulder.

Chapter 21

I t's Wednesday evening, and I am so hungry driving home. I had my first shift today in about a week and I forgot to pack myself lunch. This morning I was too preoccupied worrying about Braden meeting with Clide at 2 pm today. Hopefully, things went well and we have some more information about how to stop this drug fiasco.

Walking into my apartment, I go straight to the fridge and pull out some cheese and crackers to eat. I unpackage them and sit down on the counter. Scrolling through Instagram, I unwind after my shift. After a few minutes, I hear the door open and see Braden enter looking deflated.

"Hey."

He says, taking off his black raincoat and hanging it on my coat rack by the front door. He kicks off his shoes and walks to stand in front of me.

"Hey, how are you doing?"

I ask and pull him into a hug. He stands in between my legs and lays his head down on my shoulder in a tired way. He doesn't respond.

"I'm guessing things didn't go well with Clide?"

I ask, nervously. He shakes his head and pulls away from my arms.

"Nothing. He gave me nothing. I walked into the steakhouse, cornered him, tried to get any scrap of information, but he sat there in silence. The only word he said was "Vue" and I don't know what the hell that means. There was no trace of the old friend that I used to know."

Hopping up on the counter, Braden sits next to me and sighs. I reach over and make him a cracker with some cheese and ham on it, and hand it to him. Silently, he takes it from me and eats it.

"It's ok. I'm going over to Missy's in an hour. I'm sure she knows more information than us. Maybe "Vue" means something to her?"

Braden shakes his head and turns to look at me. I notice small tears forming in the corners of his beautiful eyes. Bringing my hands up to his face, I cradle his sharp cheeks and swipe my thumbs under his eyes to collect the tears.

"What?"

I ask worried and sympathetically. Braden shakes his head, turns forward, and crosses his arms defensively. I can see him think for a few minutes, trying to get his thoughts together.

"This is my one chance to get out of the Cynicals, so I can continue to be with you, and I'm blowing it. I need to get this information."

I place a kiss on his cheek, comforting him when I realize what he said.

"What do you mean 'So I can continue to be with you?'"

Braden clenches his jaw and slides off the counter onto the ground. Furrowing my brow in confusion, I wait for his explanation.

"Lucy, you know I love you. I want to be with you more than anything, but if I get roped back into this gang, I can't see you anymore."

Sliding off the counter to stand in front of him, I narrow my eyes.

"Can't be with me or won't be with me?"

Braden sighs and reaches for my waist, but I step out of reach.

"If I have to continue being in the gang, that means I will be off on dangerous missions with people following me and hunting me. I won't have you get hurt because of me."

Narrowing my eyes in anger, I point my finger at him and poke his chest in emphasis.

"You are not thinking straight. We have been through so much together, and we love each other. Like hell, I'm going to let you throw this away because you are being over-protective. Even if you are back in the gang, we will figure something out. I am not willing to give up on you."

I can see Braden's eyes shift from full of tension to sadness. Still, he stays silent and thoughtful. I look at the clock and realize I need to get going if I'm going to meet Missy tonight. I look back at him, and still, Braden says nothing. Angry, I grab my coat and walk to the door.

"I'm meeting Missy. Good to know how secure you feel in our relationship."

Sighing, Braden starts to say something, but I'm already out the door.

Knocking on the door of Missy's apartment on the quiet side of town, I wait for her to answer. After a few seconds, the door swings open and Missys appears with a welcoming smile.

"Hey, Lucy! Come on in."

I give her a little smile back and step inside, making sure to slip my shoes off politely. Looking around, I notice lots of books lying everywhere, a brick fireplace on the wall, black paint with dark brown accents, and a few crystals sitting in the windowsills. Missy and I sit down at her kitchen table where a few notebooks, loose-leaf paper, and her laptop sit.

"Do you want any coffee or tea? I just made myself an oat milk latte because I have a feeling we have a long night ahead of us."

I kindly decline, saying that caffeine this late in the day will mess up my sleep cycle.

"So, let's get to work. I've found a few places in the area that I think the Killers could be meeting in, but we have too many options at the moment. A few clubs, basements, and houses are on our list, but so far we have no evidence to point at any place specifically."

I nod and take a look at the list, brushing through the names quickly.

"Hmmm, none of these names sound familiar."

I say, looking around at the notebooks and papers strung about.

"Did Braden find anything while he was talking to Clide today?"

Sighing exhaustedly, I shake my head.

"He, unfortunately, got nothing. The only thing he told me was Clide mentioned the word "Vue", but that sounds like maybe he was just sniffing or sneezing.

Missy picks up on my worried body language and raises her eyebrows quizzically.

"What's up with you?"

Rolling my eyes, I lean back in the chair and play with my fingers.

"Braden and I got into a fight before I left. He wants to protect me to the point of not even being with me if he can't get out of the gang."

Missy winces and rests her elbows on the table.

"Oof, so he is one of those boyfriends. Look, I think Braden is nice and all, but if Deathface and I can be together, then I think you and your boyfriend can too."

Surprised, I lean in, intrigued.

"So, you and my brother are a thing? I kind of got the vibe but I didn't want to make things awkward by asking him."

Missy looks back at her computer and starts to type. It seems like she is trying to distract herself from this conversation.

"Your brother and I's relationship is complicated. Yes, we are together and don't see anyone else but, neither of us is too big on PDA or physical touch. We are just there for each other if that makes sense."

I nod, understanding that sometimes that emotional support outweighs the rest. Suddenly, Missy's eyes widen and she leans closer into the screen.

"I think I might have got something."

Missy hurriedly types for a few more seconds, then turns the screen around for me to see. The website on the screen is for "Mirrorball Dance Club and Bar". Missy scrolls down, and at the bottom of the webpage is a section about meeting the owner, Douglas Vue.

"That was on your list!"

She nods and turns the screen back around. After reading for a minute, her eyes light up with mischief, and she makes eye contact with me.

"Looks like they are having an event tonight that all VIPs are invited to. I bet Snake will be there."

Nodding I think for a moment, and then realize what she is getting at.

"Oh god. Missy, that is a bad idea. Braden will kill me if we go."

She chuckles and just keeps typing away at her computer, seeming to work hard on something.

"And your brother will kill me.... but this is the best way we are going to find information. We will just get in, and you can flirt it up with Snake. He won't know who you are yet. At least I don't think he will."

Rolling my eyes, I get up from the table and pace nervously.

"Oh great, thanks for that wonderfully thought-out plan. Also, how are we even going to get in there if we aren't VIPs?"

Almost on cue, Missy turns her laptop around showing a design of VIP passes on Adobe Photoshop.

"Trust me, I can get us anywhere. Now, come on. We have to change."

After an hour of trying on every sexy dress in Missy's closet later, we are finally standing in front of Mirrorball club. Dressed in a skin-tight little black dress and fishnets, I am ready to talk to the most dangerous man I've heard of, and divulge information out of him. Handing me a VIP pass, Missy checks in with me.

"How are you feeling? Are you ready to do this?"

I nod, relaxing and reminding myself I am doing this for Braden.

"Yes, I'm ready. What's the game plan?"

She pulls out her pocket mirror and adjusts her pink wig, making sure it is on her head securely.

"Once we get in, we will survey the club and go get a drink so we blend in. After we spot Snake, you need to hang out near him until you catch his eye. Believe me, you will. He has..... a type you could say."

Missy says, eying my hair and breasts. I roll my eyes and swat her shoulder.

"Then, I need you to be flirty with him. Not too much, but he might take you to a booth. If he invites you, go."

I widen my eyes, obviously looking nervous and hesitant. I am not comfortable flirting with anyone when I am in a relationship.

"Don't worry, I'll be following you the whole time. And, don't feel bad about it, you are doing it for Braden. If anything goes wrong, say you're having girl problems and need to use the restroom. Anyways, while you're with him try to ask about his career or anything you get about the Killers. Once you think you got something, leave and meet me at the back door. Deal?"

"Okay. Let's do this."

Walking up to the bouncer, we skip the general admission line and show him our VIP badges. He nods, checks our IDs, and lets us through the entrance of the club without a word. I guess Missy is who I'm contacting when I want to get Harry Styles pit tickets. Entering the club, I take in the crazy surroundings. The bottom floor is a packed dance floor with people squished together, grinding and grooving on each other. Music bumps loudly from a DJ booth elevated slightly above the dance floor, and multi-colored lights strobe the room. Above the dance floor is a balcony, I'm guessing the VIP area from the amount of security at the bottom of the stairs. From what I can see from the floor, there are booths, tables, and poles that some women and men are dancing on.

Missy pats my shoulder and points towards the bar on the side of the room. I nod at her, getting her signal, and we walk over to the bar to get a drink. I, of course, order a long island iced tea while Missy orders a tequila shot. While we wait for our drinks, I scan the VIP area, looking for anyone suspicious or dangerous. Finally, in the corner, I see him. An extremely tall and buff man is leaning against the railing with a glass in his hand, scanning the dancefloor. With his white button-down open halfway down his chest, I can see the large number of tattoos littering his skin. Examining his face, he looks thoughtful but calculated. Missy hands me my drink and whispers in my ear,

"Go up there and stand by the railing, sipping your drink."

Nodding, I wrap my fingers around my drink and make my way to the bottom of the stairs. The bouncer at the bottom again, asks for my VIP pass, and I show it to him confidently. After a few seconds, the man stands to the side and lets me climb up the stairs to the second-floor overlook. Nerves rush through my system, but I shift my focus elsewhere. I need to do this well. Once I am up the stairs, I make a show of looking around the overlook, watching the dancers on the small stage, and then incon-spicuously taking a sexy stance a few feet down from Snake at the railing. I see him notice me out of the corner of my eye, and I try not to tense up. Instead, I take a sip of my drink, brush my hair to the side, and arch my back. This seems to do the trick as he slowly saunters over to me and leans his elbow on the railing beside my body.

"What's a pretty thing like you doing up here alone?"

His breath hits my ear and causes sickly, slimy tingles to go down my spine. I have never felt this much negative energy just from meeting a man. Swallowing my disgust, I paste an airheaded, unbothered smile on my face, and turn towards him.

"I was supposed to meet my friend, but I think she got caught up."

I make a fake pouty face and take another sip of my drink.

"Well, we can be friends if you want."

Holding back my laughter at that embarrassing comment, I quirk my head to the side and raise one eyebrow.

"Friends? But I don't even know you."

He smiles and takes his hand in his, bringing it up to his lips, kissing the back of it.

"My name's Snake, and I come here often. And you are?"

I nervously rack my brain to come up with a fake name and blurt out the first one that comes to mind.

"Belle Moods."

Facepalming myself in my mind, I try to paste an innocent look on my face. Apparently, it works, as he leans back into me.

"Belle, why don't we sit down, and we can get to know each other better."

Nodding, I let him place his sweaty hand on the small of my back and lead me to a dimly lit booth at the side of the balcony. I try to sit as far away from him as possible, but close enough he won't get suspicious.

"So, my Belle, tell me about yourself."

Snake asks while sipping his drink and making a horrible attempt at seductive eyes. Playing with my hair, and biting my lip to the best of my ability, I explain an impromptu cover story.

"I'm currently a graduate student at Washington State, but I'm on fall break. What about you, what do you do?"

Snake raises his eyebrows at my question but lets it slide.

"I am a...... project manager, you could say. I come up with plans, and my team performs them."

Pretending to be interested, I lean forward towards him.

"Wow, you have a team that works for you? So you're the boss?"

He lights up as I embarrassingly inflate his ego.

"Yes, I manage a group of twelve men. I am the boss of all of them, and I own everything the..... Company has."

Sliding his hand under the table, Snake places it on my knee. The feeling of his sweaty and heavy hand on me makes my skin crawl, but I push the feeling aside.

"Wow, that's so -----"

Snake's phone rings, interrupting my sentence. He sighs and digs out his phone and wallet from his back pocket. Placing his wallet on the table, he puts his phone up to his ear and answers it.

"Hello? Yes. No. What?"

Snake takes his gross hand off me and turns away from me for privacy. I take this opportunity to closely examine his wallet for any hints or clues. At first glance, nothing stands out. He just has a black leather wallet with his name printed on the front, and the edges slightly faded. But, just to the side, I can see the jagged end of a key sticking slightly out of the wallet. Without thinking, I reach forward, sneakily take it out of the wallet, and tuck it in my bra. By the time Snake turns back around, I am already crafting my story on how I am going to get out of this.

"Hey, I have to go. My friend texted and said she's at a different club."

Snake's eyes narrow suspiciously, but before he can reach for me, I have slid out of the booth and am trekking down the stairs. Back door, back door, where's the back door?

Taking a glance behind me, I see Snake staring at me angrily from the balcony, still sipping his drink. Suddenly, I collide with someone forcefully.

"Sorry..."

I say, not seeing who it is. I grab my purse from the floor and stand up to see who I bumped into. Relieved to see it's Missy, I quickly usher her down the hallway to the door.

"Missy! Thank God. We have to go. I got something and I think Snake is suspicious."

Missy nods and we speed up, practically running. As soon as we push the metal bar to swing open the door though, we are met with Braden and Dave's angry faces.

Chapter 22

Missy and I hesitate for just a second, realizing that Braden and Dave found us at the club. Dave is crossing his arms in a tensed fashion, staring down at us while Braden has a mix of worry and anger on his face. Surprised and furious, Dave asks,

"What the hell are you two doing here?"

I'm about to answer, but Missy grabs my arm, pulling me along and completely ignoring Dave's question.

"We don't have time to talk, we need to get to the car now."

I hear the boys start to run behind us, and we quickly cross the street and all enter Missy's car. Missy hops on the driver's side, and I try to get into the passenger side when my brother grabs my arm.

"Get in the back, Lucy. I need to be upfront."

Again, before I can cuss at him, Missy leans over, slaps his hand away from my arm, and pulls me into the car. While I buckle up, I hear her scolding him.

"You don't deserve the fucking front seat Death. While you two were sitting on your asses at home, Lucy and I actually got shit done. Sit in the back."

With that, I give him a shit-eating smile and close the door. Grumbling, Dave goes to sit in the back seat next to Braden. Braden hasn't said much at all, but with one look back, I can tell he is not happy with us.

"Can we go back to yours, Lucy?"

Missy asks while merging onto the freeway.

"Sure, do you need directions?"

Missy nods. I reach over, take her phone out of her jacket pocket, attach it to the car system, and plug in my address. The way home is tense and silent. I can tell the two in the back are angry at us but don't want to talk to us while they can't look us in the face. I know where they are coming from, they want us to be safe. But, I wanted to do something to help. If using my charms to get an important key and a regular location of the gang is the best way I can help, I don't feel bad one bit.

Finally, all of us arrive at the apartment complex and we all take the elevator up. As soon as I have the door unlocked and we are inside, Dave and Braden look at us angrily.

"What do you think you were doing going to that club? I saw all their bikes outside, all of the Killer's members were there. Also, to keep it a secret from me and Deathface? What the hell?!"

Braden says stormily, pulling at his dark hair and pacing around the kitchen anxiously.

"Braden, it was fine. Nothing happened. When I talked to Snake he didn't-"

"You talked to Snake?!?"

Dave yells out in surprise. Braden freezes his walking and flips his head towards me.

"That is the stupidest thing you could have done. What if he knew you were associated with us? He would have killed you on the spot. I can't believe you dared to talk to him."

Dave scolds me angrily, waving a finger at me.

"Damn right she had the audacity. Don't talk to Lucy that way, she is ballsy and it paid off. Also, why the hell were you two there?"

Dave rolls his eyes and crosses his arms. I came to your apartment to check on how things were going but nobody was home. Your laptop was left open on the table with the club name on it, and I just knew you two went. I grabbed Braden and we got a cab to come get you."

Missy sighs and rubs her temple.

"Look, Nothing happened. She was careful and got us more information than any of you assholes have gotten."

Missy backs me up, taking a step towards Dave. With the mention of me finding information, both Dave and Braden's attention turned to me.

"I know how risky that was, but it was my decision. In the end, we got the information we needed."

Reaching down, I pull the small silver key out from where I previously tucked it in my bra, and show all of them.

"This was tucked in Snake's wallet. We were sitting in a booth, and he had to take a call. I grabbed it, tucked it into my bra, and ducked out of there as quickly as possible. It seems important."

Braden takes a step forward and wraps his arms around me anxiously. I can tell he has calmed down a little bit, and now he is more nervous than mad.

"Did anything happen to you? Did he touch you at all?"

I reciprocate the hug, resting my forehead against his chest and taking in his calming scent. I guess he forgot about our little squabble earlier.

"No, it happened pretty fast and he didn't really touch me. He just rested his hand on my knee which felt a little weird."

I can feel his body tense up at the end, but I rub his back gently, letting him know that I am okay.

"Lucy, can I see that key? Also, can I borrow your laptop?"

Missy asks. I break away from Braden's arms and pass her the silver key. She sits down at the kitchen table and I open my laptop sitting on the counter and bring it to her. Immediately, she starts typing away, finding out information.

Braden stands next to me and wraps his warm arm around me, kissing the top of my head a few times. It feels so good.

"It looks like this key is attached to the front entrance of this building. It looks like a warehouse of some sort. Does this building look familiar?"

Missy turns the laptop around, showing us a photo of a white boxy warehouse with a white van parked in front.

I hear Dave gasp in excitement and take a few steps closer, examining the laptop.

"No way."

"What?"

I say, intrigued.

"Snake used to work out of here when he was younger, it got torn down a long time ago. I should have known he would have returned to it."

Missy turns the laptop back around and does some more typing.

"Can we get some spies to either infiltrate or watch the building for a few days? See who comes in and out?"

Braden nods and excuses himself into my bedroom to make a few calls.

"It's weird though, there are two addresses that connect to this building, one in North Seattle and one in East. When I try to look up the address in North Seattle, no pictures come up. Maybe we can get someone to look into that too."

Missy says while resting her head on her hand. Dave nods and walks a few steps until he is behind her, peering at the laptop. He leans down to her ear and whispers something, making Missy lean closer into him. It looks intimate, whatever they are talking about so I turn to see what Braden is up to. Just as I turn around though, he is coming out of my room looking tired.

"I called a few members, they have assignments we will know in a few days who is going in and out, as well as what times."

I hear my laptop shut and Missy gets up from the table, getting her car keys from her pocket.

"Okay, let's meet Friday night? We can make a game plan then."

Dave and Braden nod. I hug Missy and thank her for watching out for me tonight. I love how supportive she is. Dave gives me a long glance before they walk out together that I can't read. I can't tell if he is sorry, regretful, or still mad at me.

"Lucy."

Turning to face him, a look of worry is painted across his face.

"Can we talk about our fight?"

Looking into his eyes I don't say anything but cue him to continue with a slight tilt of the head.

"I want to apologize for this morning. I got too nervous that if I didn't get that information, I could never see you again and I freaked out. Even if I wind up back in the gang permanently, I still want you. But my question is will you still want me?"

Shaking my head in disbelief, I wrap my arms around him gently.

"Yes, of course, I will still want you. I just need you to talk to me when you get nervous and anxious. If you do that, we can get through it together.

Braden takes a minute to stare into my eyes passionately and then he leans down to connect our lips.

"My love"

I whisper into the kiss emotionally. Braden groans huskily, wrapping his arms around my ass and legs, and leads me into my bedroom. Shutting the door behind us with his foot, Braden lays me down on the bed passionately. Bunching up the back of his shirt, I claw at him to take it off. He excitedly slips it off and tosses it to the side of the room. He pushes up my sexy party dress around my chest and kneels in between them to connect our lips again. Slipping some tongue into his mouth, I start to take control of the kiss letting him know who is boss. Gathering even more courage, I wrap my leg around his waist and turn us so that I'm on top. Braden is surprised and grasps my body closer to him. Reaching down to his jeans, I unbutton the top and slowly unzip them. Suddenly, Braden sits up with me still on him. Now I am straddling his right leg, my breasts pressed up against his chest.

"You want to be in control huh?"

Braden starts to kiss my neck wildly, slightly nipping the sides of it. I lean my head back, fully enjoying the feeling.

"But I'm going to have to override that. Baby, ride my thigh."

My heart skips a beat at the thought. I've never done that before.

"Huh?"

Braden pulls down the strap of my dress exposing my breasts. He leans down to capture one of nipples in his mouth, sucking amazingly. I let out a moan, biting my lip.

"I want you to come on my thigh. Ride me."

Braden places his large hands on my ass, grinding me up and down on his rough jean-clad thigh. The friction feels so amazing, I can't help but continue the action, grinding my clit on him.

He continues to suck my nipples into his mouth, altering between the two making sure to stimulate them with his tongue and teeth.

"Yes!"

I moan out, feeling a knot build in my abdomen. My legs start to shake and I pick up my pace, grinding feverishly on his thigh.

Reaching behind me, Braden gives my ass a firm spank, then forcefully rubs my clit against himself.

"Just like that baby."

Feeling myself fall over the edge, I lace my hands in his hair and curve my back in response, pressing against him. I can feel the wetness I've created sitting on top of his thigh as I begin to recover from my orgasm.

I am still reeling from my high when I connect our lips again, enjoying the taste of his lips, reaching down to his jeans, I grasp his cock from the inside of his boxers and pump him a few times. I notice and enjoy how his abs tense and flex every time I run my hand over his shaft. Ignoring what he said earlier, I take control and press his chest down against the bed so I have full access to him. Braden starts to protest but I shut him up when I wrap my lips around his tip, sucking. Circling my tongue around the top, I make him moan underneath me. Playing with his balls, I ease my mouth down, enveloping most of his shaft into my hot, wet, mouth.

"Ah fuck"

He tensed a little and weaves his fingers into my hair. I alternate between fondling his balls and passionately sucking him until he is trembling underneath me.

"Baby I'm going to come."

Taking that as encouragement, I increase my pace, taking his length all the way down my throat. Gagging, I suck on him harder, making his legs tighten. Seconds later, I hear him gasp, and wet liquid comes shooting down my throat. Swallowing the come up, I take him out of my mouth and lick his cock, cleaning up any more white liquid.

Reaching for me, Braden presses me against his body, peppering small kisses all over my face. I wrap my arms around him, enjoying his warm embrace.

"You're incredible baby."

That night I slept well, knowing that Braden and I were on good terms and in love with each other.

Chapter 23

A few days later, I'm hanging out with Missy at her favorite coffee shop The Bean Machine, going over plans to infiltrate the Killer's hideout and destroy all of the deadly drugs. The place has a warm ambiance with a crackling fire, Taylor Swift records playing, and a black cat sleeping on the wood windowsill. Sipping my chai, I gaze over a floorplan of the warehouse that one of Braden's spies must have recorded.

"So, where do we even begin? Is infiltrating the best idea?"

I ask. Missy pushes her black frames up her nose and uncaps a pen, preparing it for use.

"I really don't know how else we would have the chance to destroy the product. Trying to get rid of it right before they distribute it would be very risky. Some of it still could get onto the streets."

Nodding, I bite my lip trying to think of another idea.

"What if we set up a fake buyer? They want to see and purchase all the coke at a different location than the warehouse. Then, while they transfer it, we could destroy the truck or shipping container."

Missy thinks about my idea for a minute and takes a sip of her coffee. A few seconds pass and she makes a frustrated sound.

"No, that will never work. Even if we convince a buyer that they have worked with

before to help us, Snake wouldn't go for it. Not with how valuable this cocaine is."

"Shit."

I say, racking my empty brain for any ideas. Scanning the floorplan of the warehouse, I

try to imagine where they would be keeping the drugs. Questioning, I ask,

"Are you sure it's all in here? What about the other address?"

Missy shakes her head.

"Yes, Braden said everything is at this address. The Killers also meet at the other one but it's mostly for hangouts and meetings. No shit goes down over there apparently."

Just as the bell on the front door of the coffee shop rings, I get an idea.

"What if we were invited in? Then they would be unsuspecting that we would cause trouble. Less security and easy access."

Missy's eyebrows shoot up in surprise.

"Lucy, that's a great idea! What did you have in mind?"

"What's a great idea?"

Braden says while walking over to our secluded table and taking a seat next to me. My brother is following along behind him, a pensive look on his face. I give Braden a brief but genuine hug, loving the soft flannel he is wearing today. Braden and I had a talk yesterday about me continuing to help with this gang issue. Surprisingly, it was a very open talk where both of us listened and understood one another. He shared his worries about me being involved and I told him that we were a package deal. If he has to be in this mess, so do I. We came to an agreement that I can help with any planning or communications, and the actual gang will deal with the conflict.

"What if we tricked them into thinking we wanted to collaborate with them? Get them to invite us into their warehouse for a conversation, and then blow the storage up. With only a few people in the meeting, we would know what we are walking into."

Dave sighs heavily, absentmindedly leaning back in his chair and wrapping his arm around Missy. She gives him the side-eye but chooses to ignore it.

"I hate the idea of even pretending to work with The Killers, but yes. I think it would work. Snake would hate to admit it, but he has always been jealous of my gang. Offering him an opportunity to be in charge of both is something he would have to explore."

Braden reaches under the table, giving my leg a supportive squeeze. I look over to him and blush.

"We would have to do this soon though, in about two days' time. They are planning on distributing this shit in a week."

Braden says, still looking me in the eyes.

"How should we destroy the coke? Explosives? Fire?"

I ask.

"Fire. Definitely fire. Explosives would get too many people's attention, a.k.a the police. A fire we can cover-up, especially in a forgotten place like that warehouse."

Resting my head against Braden's shoulder I tense at the idea of the police getting involved.

"Who would contact them about setting up a meeting?"

Dave makes eye contact with me.

"I have to do it. Snake won't trust anyone else's offer."

I raise my eyebrow in a questioning manner.

"What makes you so sure he is going to say yes?"

Smiling apprehensively, Dave leans forward towards me.

"We have someone he especially wants to see again. I think luring him in with the possibility of seeing you again and the gangs collaborating is an offer he can't pass up."

Braden straightens his spine rigidly.

"Woah Woah Woah. Lucy, I am fine with you planning and being involved but going to this meeting where fire will be involved is not a good idea. Deathface, I thought you were on my side!"

Dave rolls his eyes and relaxes back in his seat again.

"I've already thought about that. We will just have someone rush her out of the building before anything happens. She goes, says a short hello to Snake, then bails. She will be safe, I wouldn't let her go if I was worried."

Braden stays tense but nods slowly in agreement.

"I still hate the fact that he wants to see my girlfriend again. I don't like flaunting around Lucy just to get the shit we need."

I reach under the table and grab his hand comfortingly.

"It's okay. Nothing will happen and if this is what I have to do in order for this meeting to happen, I can do it."

Braden makes eye contact with me, searching for any hesitancy or doubt in my expression. When he finds nothing, he sighs and turns back to Missy and Dave.

"Fine. But Lucy's getting in and out. No dallying. I want her escort to be prompt and armed."

Nodding, Dave agrees.

"Believe me, I'm making sure she is perfectly safe. If even I can let her go into this meeting, you can too."

Just a few weeks ago I remember Dave being so overprotective. I asked Missy to talk to him about it, and I guess it worked. Even if he is still protective, he has loosened the reins a little and I couldn't be more glad.

"Okay, Dave, write to Snake proposing a meeting in a few days. As soon as we hear back, I'll let you two know the time, date, and plan."

Chugging the rest of my chai, I set it down on the table and pull on my coat. It's freezing this November and the temperature has made me start wearing my puffy jacket everywhere I go. After giving my brother and Missy a hug, Braden and I slip out of the cozy coffee shop into the pouring rain. We run to the car, hand in hand, trying to avoid getting drenched. I unlock the car and both of us slip inside.

"Thanks for driving me home Luce. Meetings were horrible today, the whole gang is super anxious about this laced coke."

I lean over and give him a chaste kiss, enjoying the little drops of water that are brushing his face.

Turning the key in the ignition, I pull out of the parking lot and start driving.

"Of course. I'm sorry meetings were bad, that's sucky. I had an okay day but nothing too exciting happened at work. Mostly just treating the flu season."

While driving, Braden continually presses small kisses to my hand, fingers, and wrist. The feeling of his slightly wet lips on my skin sends shivers down my spine.

"Wait, where are you going? The turn home was back there."

I smile discreetly and adjust in my seat.

"Oh, nowhere. Just a little surprise."

Stealing a glance over at him, I see his eyebrow raise suspiciously.

"A surprise? For what?"

I wink at him and pull into a parking spot on the side of the road.

"You know what!"

We both get out of the car and link hands as I lead him down the street. Pretty soon, the Salt & Straw sign pops into view and Braden laughs sweetly.

"Happy Birthday Braden!! I know you tried to hide your birthday from me, but I figured it out and want to do something special to celebrate!"

Even under the streetlight, I can see a strong blush making its way onto his cheeks. When we get in line, Braden wraps me up in his arms and gives me a sweet kiss to show appreciation. I can tell he is holding back, but we are in public. A group of teens is right behind us and I would rather not have eyes on us while we make out. Once we get up to the sampling area, Braden tells the nice worker that he would like to try the cookie dough, pear & blue cheese, and snickerdoodle ice cream flavors. He puts the little tasting spoons in his mouth, tasting each flavor and deciding which one he likes the most.

"Snickerdoodle is really good baby, you should definitely try that one. Actually, surprisingly, pear & blue cheese is not that bad!"

I laugh and make a face of disgust at that kind of flavor, but decide to try it anyway.

"Ok, you're right. It's not that bad but it's not my fave."

I end up choosing peppermint cocoa, the Christmas flavor that was just released. Both of us get our ice cream in a waffle cone and walk to the register. I pay and give the workers a tip, thanking them for the really good samples. Braden and I walk over to an empty table and sit down, bodies brushing against each other.

"Thank you for this Lucy. It's so sweet of you to take me out for ice cream."

I press a kiss to his cheek and smile at him.

"It's your birthday! We have to do something special. I knew if I got you a gift you would maybe feel embarrassed, especially since you didn't tell me about today. I thought going to get ice cream would be a better alternative."

Braden sighs and takes a few more licks of his ice cream.

"I-I wanted to tell you. But, I haven't really had someone special to share birthdays with before. Having you in my life is still new, even if we have been seeing each other for a couple of months now."

Nodding, I run my non-sticky hand through his hair, comforting him.

"I understand, and really, it's okay. I just want to be able to make you feel special."

He smiles at me gratefully and kisses me again, this time more passionately. His hand squeezes my leg, sending warmth to my core.

"You do. You always make me feel special."

"It's still your birthday, is there anything else you want today?"

He eats the last bite of his waffle cone, licks his fingers with a heated gaze pointed towards me, and pulls me into him by my jacket.

"I can think of a few things I want, none of those things I can have right here though."

He breathes seductively onto my lips. That night, we go home and I pleasure him until we fall asleep. Every time Braden tries to return the favor or make me feel good, I flip him under me and continue my ministrations. Usually, I hate giving head to a guy or making him the center of attention during sex because, in my past, that choice is usually begged for or coerced. With Braden, he never asks for anything, which makes me love him more. I never thought I would have it, but finally, at the age of 24, I have a healthy, safe, and loving sex life. I deserve it and I'm happy, especially for my younger self. I went through so much with my ex, and it feels great to be in such an amazing relationship.

Chapter 24

"Is this everyone?"

I ask, looking around the Cynical's house. Missy, Dave, Braden, and a few other large-looking men have gathered in the main room to go over the plan. It's so weird to be back here, and honestly, I'm feeling on edge. Memories of the last time I was here flood my mind and nervous energy flows through my body.

"I think so. Now, let's go over the plan."

Missy sits down on the couch and points to the map of the warehouse sitting on the coffee table. Everyone scooches closer to the map, making sure they can see clearly.

"The meeting with Snake is at 8 pm tonight. We will meet him in the main area, with at least a few guards."

Dave explains directly.

"At first, only me, Agent, Lucy, and Siko will go in. If we have too many of us go, it will look like an ambush. I have a body camera hidden in my jacket that Missy can see from the car. If we need the rest of you, Missy will send you in. Hopefully, this will be a smooth and easy plan, no missteps."

He continues, crossing his arms over his chest.

"Once you five go in, Lucy will greet Snake quickly, then head out. Siko, I want your attention to fully be on keeping Lucy safe. Have your gun at your side the whole time and keep her by you. Hopefully, Death, you can distract him enough for her to slip out easily. While we distract Snake, Devil will slip out of the van, and enter through the side door with the key. After a few days of Agent's spying, we know that all of the coke is being held in this room."

Missy explains while pointing to the room behind the balcony overlooking the main room.

"It might be hard to slip into here unnoticed, but if Death can keep everyone concentrated on the meeting, things will go according to plan. In Devil's backpack, there is a jug of gasoline and a lighter."

I look over to Devil, who is leaning smugly against the window at the side of the room. His icy blonde hair is shaved on one side, he has a few face piercings, and his all-black leather outfit contributes to his bad-boy persona. He catches me looking at him and he bows his head quickly out of respect. Awkwardly, I look away and check on Braden. He has been standing next to me the whole time, fully focused on the map Missy is pointing to. This morning he made me wear a fully fireproof jacket and pants, "just in case". I have full confidence that we will be able to accomplish this plan, but I put it on just to make him feel better.

"After I receive confirmation that Devil is about to blow up all the coke, I will let Death know through the small mic in his ear. He will make an excuse, make sure everyone, including the other gang, clears out, and then kaboom! The streets are safe."

Nodding, I go over the plan again in my head. Of course, there are a ton of things that could go wrong, but it's worth it. If we don't get rid of all those drugs, so many people will be killed.

"This plan sounds good. Are we forgetting anything?"

I ask, wrapping an arm around Braden for comfort. He pulls me in closer to him and relaxes at the touch. Everyone thinks for a minute and shakes their heads no.

"It looks like we have an hour until the meeting. Let's go. Now."

Dave says while looking every member in the eye firmly and then walking out of the room. Missy just rolls her eyes, picks up the map, and follows Dave.

"How are you feeling?"

Braden whispers to me. I look up at him warmly and squeeze his hand.

"I'm feeling good. Nervous of course, but confident."

He shakes his head and gives me a small hug. I can tell he is anxious by the tightness in his shoulders.

"Lucy, if you don't want to do this, please tell me. You can walk out of here, just say the word."

"No, no. I have to do this. We have to do this. How can we walk away knowing we didn't do everything we could to help this cause. And, if we do this, you and I can never be associated with the Cynicals again."

Braden sighs and nods his head nervously. I kiss him on the cheek and walk into the kitchen where everyone is zipping up backpacks, lacing up boots, and strapping guns to their hips. It feels weird to be in this environment, but I remind myself that this is a one-time thing. Hopefully. After everyone is packed and prepped, we all pile into the black windowless van and head off.

Pulling up to the warehouse, I immediately get an ominous vibe. The outside walls are a mix of white with grey industrial piping around the edges of the building. Dumpsters litter the sides and an almost empty and dark parking lot is spread in front. The only way to see the door is from the light of the lone, flickering streetlight.

Missy turns around from the passenger seat and looks at all of us cramped in the back of the van. I am squished between Siko, Devil, and sitting on Braden's lap simultaneously. I barely take in how uncomfortable this seating arrangement is because of the intensity of my anxious, beating heart.

Thump. Thump. Thump.

"It's time."

Missy says, making eye contact with each of us, and then stops on me. I see the littlest flare of fear, but it disappears as fast as it came. Lastly, she connects her eyes with Dave who is driving, and gives him a wink. Braden swings open the door and gets out first. I am about to follow him when Siko holds back my arm and makes me wait until he is outside of the car before I exit. Now looking at the door, two people dressed in all black are standing on either side with their arms crossed.

"Let's go."

Dave says, gesturing to our group to follow him. Walking up, he puts on the most serious and unreadable expression I have ever seen him wear. He is here to get done with business. When we pass through the door of the warehouse, our three guys are positioned in a vee with me awkwardly in the middle of it. I make eye contact with one of Snake's men standing at the door, and plaster on my best version of the expression Dave wears. Inside,

Snake is sitting at a dark, hickory desk stationed smack in the middle of the concrete and wood warehouse. Random couches, desks, and chairs litter the spacious room. One chair is laid out in front of his desk, and some sort of stapled stack of papers rests on the desktop.

"Deathface, you're here."

Snake says from his relaxed position, of his crossed feet resting on the top of the desk. The smirk he wears is dark but curious at the same time, sending my skin crawling. Looking around, I notice four guards standing about.

"I'm prompt."

Dave says standing in front of the desk, confidently looking straight at Snake.

"So, about this proposal, why would you ever give me your men? I never thought you were very smart but I never took you as stupid."

Dave's jaw tightens just the slightest bit, but other than that he impressively keeps himself composed. The one thing my brother has is his ego, but he is doing a great job keeping himself in check while it is being questioned.

"I have new priorities in life, and running a gang isn't one of them."

Snake shifts focus to Braden and smiles a crusty, toothy smile.

"Doesn't that piss you off Agent? He just doesn't feel like being in charge anymore so he passes it all off to me. Not to you."

Braden doesn't respond, he keeps looking stoically in front of himself. He is so grounded that it makes me wonder if he even heard Snake's words.

"Shut up Snake and let's get to the signing."

Dave sits down on the chair, grabs the contract, and starts to read through it nonchalantly. Little does my brother know that as soon as he sits down in the chair, Snake sees me for the first time. His eyebrows lift and his disgustingly creepy smirk reappears on his face.

"Ah, you brought me a treat. How kind of you Deathface."

Dave looks up from the contract, scowls at Snake, but chooses to ignore his comment.

"This looks fine. Where's a pen?"

Snake hands him a pen but keeps his heated eyes trained on me. They roam up and down my body in a sickening manner. Multiple times his eyes stop on my breasts and I have to stop myself from crossing my arms over them. Masking my uneasiness, I again put on an unbothered expression. Dave signs the contract and sets it down on the desk.

"Now, I think it's time for her to leave. Say goodbye, Snake."

Without another thought I walk quickly towards the door, Siko leading the way. I'm almost to the exit when Snake's arm blocks my path.

"No. You are not leaving. You, little sexy, are staying."

Holding down my vomit at the nickname he called me, I take a few steps away from him but stay in the corner of the room. Missy said it might go like this. I'll stay by the exit so I can slip out before the fire starts. Reaching up to my face, Snake presses a finger under my jaw and raises my head so that I have no choice but to look at him.

"Good girl."

He whispers. My stomach sinks but I stay quiet, not wanting to make him suspect anything. I hear a soft rustling in the background but think nothing of it. All I can focus on is keeping my unbothered expression on.

"Snake get your ass over here and sign this."

Dave yells, annoyed. Snake lets go of my chin and saunters over to the desk. Braden sneakily checks me over with his eyes, making sure I'm ok. I give him a discreet nod, trying to comfort him. He looks furious, but hopefully, he can continue to keep himself in check.

Without even looking twice at the contract, Snake signs the bottom line with a frilly signature and a smirk.

BANG.

A startling gunshot booms through the room and we all turn towards the sound. Shit. Devil falls to the ground dead while one of Snake's members blows off the smoke from his gun.

"What the hell is this! What the hell are you pulling!"

Snake yells furiously, pulling out his gun and aiming it at Dave. Dave immediately arms himself pointing the gun right back at Snake. Every one of Snake's gang members runs behind Snake creating a wall.

"Get the fuck out of here now Lucy."

Siko yells to me and gestures towards the exit door that is only a few feet away from me. He runs over to where Braden and Dave are standing and pulls out his gun.

"You don't know what you've done, Deathface."

Snake pulls his trigger, but Dave is too fast, the three of them dodge loud, whirling bullets, diving behind various furniture. As soon as they take cover, they poke out their guns from behind the furniture and fire back.

I need to leave. Nobody is looking at me, now is my time to run. Wait, no one remembers I'm here. And the coke is still up there, untouched.

Without thinking twice, I hurriedly run up the stairs as quietly as I can. When I reach Devil's dead body, I try not to look into his still open eyes and instead slip his backpack off of him. I've seen death before at my job, but not recently. Even in this dark and eerie warehouse where I'm making the riskiest decision of my life, I know I will never forget this death.

Unzipping the backpack as I run across the balcony to the room on the right side, I take out the lighter and gasoline, unscrewing the cap feverishly. The metal cap falls to the ground, gasoline leaks everywhere, and the cap's bang on the concrete can be heard through the warehouse. Shit.

I see Snake quickly turn around and glare at me, aiming his gun.

"You bitch!"

Jumping to the right I dodge the bullet, hearing it go whirling past me. Sprinting into the room, I slide open the top of the huge wooden crate in the center of the room. Revealed are hundreds of little plastic bags of coke. Hurriedly, I dump the gasoline all over the bags, making sure to get some everywhere. Dropping the gasoline, I reach for the lighter. As soon as I turn it on and throw it, this whole room will go up in flames. My thoughts are all jumbled and I can barely think straight as I yell,

"Get the fuck out"

Dazed, I turn around, turn on the lighter, throw it into the crate, and make a beeline out of the room.

BOOM

The room erupts in flames and a searing pain slices through my legs. Orange and red blur cover the walls, and smoke fogs up my vision making it hard to see anything. Breathing feels impossible. Rushing to get out of the huge fire that engulfs everywhere I look, I run straight outside the room and through what feels like wood. Suddenly, I am falling through the air, head spinning.

The next thing I know, I hear a crack and my vision goes dark.

Chapter 25

Discomfort. That's the feeling I wake up to. My lower legs and ankles are stinging horribly. Every time I move them and they brush against the sheets, the pain becomes sharper. I rub my eyes slowly, letting them adjust to the harsh lights surrounding me.

"Lucy, you're awake."

Braden wraps his comforting hand around mine and places a small kiss on the back of it.

"My legs hurt.."

I mumble out and try to sit up groggily.

"Wait, stay where you are, I'll go get the nurse and tell her you're up."

Braden says, sitting next to me. His hair looks disheveled and he is in the same outfit he was in when everything went up in flames, literally. Getting up from the chair, he swiftly leaves the hospital room on a mission.

"Wha-how long have I been here?"

I ask anxiously, trying to sit up again. Dave stands up from his chair across from me and sits in the empty chair Braden just left. He carefully pushes me back into the hospital bed pillows and wipes away the strands of hair stuck to my cheeks.

"Shhh, you're ok, everything's ok. You've been out for about a day. When you fell, you hit your head on the concrete. Thankfully, you landed feet first, so the hit was not as bad as it could have been."

"I didn't mean to fall, I was just trying to get out of there as fast as I could. I guess I hit that railing?"

Dave nods and smiles sadly.

"You didn't just hit it, Lucy, you broke through it and fell about 10 feet."

My heart skips a beat.

"10 feet! Jesus, no wonder my legs hurt like hell."

Dave crosses his arms and leans back in the chair.

"Sure, your legs are hurt from that impact, but your ankles are burnt up from the fire. Thank God that boyfriend of yours made you wear that fireproof suit, I don't want to think of what could've happened if you... if you weren't."

Dave avoids eye contact and bites his cheek, stumbling on his words. Reaching out I take his hand in mine and calm him down.

"Hey, it's ok now. I burned all of the drugs, there's no way that they can get out on the streets now. Honestly, knowing that is what is keeping me sane right now."

Dave nods, looking towards the door. He's probably wondering where Braden is with the nurse.

"Although, I don't know if things are back to being safe now with all your men in the hands of Snake. Please tell me that you didn't sign Braden away too with that contract."

I say nervously. If Braden is now with Snake, there's no way he is ever going to get out of this job and get to focus on other things. I bet Snake will make his life a living hell. A grin slowly stretches out onto Dave's face and he relaxes back into the chair with a look of pride.

"What?"

I ask, confused. Dave hesitates.

"What!"

"Lucy, I tricked Snake. Did you notice how he walked away for a minute in between me signing and him signing?"

I nod, not seeing where this is going.

"Snake signed the contract, Dave. I saw it, all your men-"

"I switched the contract."

Dave interrupts me, smirking.

"I switched the contract he gave me for one that Missy wrote a few days ago. One I pre-signed. When he came back from looking at you, I hated that by the way, he didn't even notice that I switched them. He signed it without a second look."

Sitting up again in astonishment, I realize what he did. Holy shit...

"Wait, so what does that mean? What did you get from Snake?"

Dave frowns and pushes me back down on the bed, annoyed.

"Jesus, can you stop sitting up please!"

I giggle. Sometimes the greatest joy in a little sister's life is annoying her big brother.

"The contract that Snake signed says that he will resign from his position of the gang leader, and all assets, including men, will go to me. He has to follow it too. Contracts are highly respected in the industry. If you sign, you have to go through with it. "

"No way."

I breathe out, astonished. It's over. This gang rivalry, the crazy danger, it's over. Sure, there's still going to be people on edge and guns in Braden and I's life, but they will be all under Dave's control.

"I can't believe-"

"Lucy, here's the nurse!"

Braden walks into the room with a nurse following quickly behind him. The nurse walks up to my bedside and starts to evaluate my vitals, writing something on his clipboard. I can't help a huge smile forming on my face as I look at Braden.

"Come here, come here, come here!!"

I yell at Braden excitedly, reaching out my arms for him to hug me in celebration. A small, relieved smile forms on his face. Reaching down, his warm arms wrap around me comfortingly, and he places a kiss on my forehead.

"Dave told you huh? It's all over."

Nodding into his chest, I enjoy the peaceful feeling that surrounds us. Even though my legs are burning, and I am still in the hospital, I see hope and happiness in our future.

I spend about a week in the hospital, recovering from the head trauma and the second-degree burns on my ankles. I try to catch up on work, answer emails, and let everyone know that I will be back in a few weeks, but no one leaves me alone enough for me to be productive. Braden stays by my side 24/7 unless he is working, Dave makes sure to scold me multiple times for almost killing myself, and Missy makes sure to bring me iced chai's every morning. Although, the greatest joy this week was seeing Kiera and Michelle. The first time they were let into my room to visit, it made my whole day. Kiera ran up to my bedside, yanking Michelle behind her, and gave me a ton of slobbery kisses all over my cheeks and forehead. Not to mention that she snuck wine into the hospital.

Feeling peaceful is something I am getting accustomed to now. Out of the hospital, life has felt like a dream. Going back to work full time and getting to see my patients, staying at Braden's almost every night, spending quality time with Kiera, Michelle, and Rufus have been my highlights. Everything feels at peace.

Ding Dong

The doorbell rings and Rufus immediately starts barking and running to the door. Getting up from where I am reflecting over these past few weeks on the couch, I head towards the front door, expecting it to be Braden. He gets off around this time and we usually hang out and.... stuff before Kiera and Michelle get home from work. Pulling open the door, I say,

"Hey, you know you can just come in-"

Nobody is there. Weird.

Looking around the hallway, I see nothing, it's normal except one ominously flickering lamp at the end of the hall near the elevator. I am about to retreat inside until I see it. Someone has left a note for me on the ground in front of the door.

Lucy,

If you think I am out of your life, think again. I might not have my men or my status, but I have drive. I am coming after you.

- S

THE END